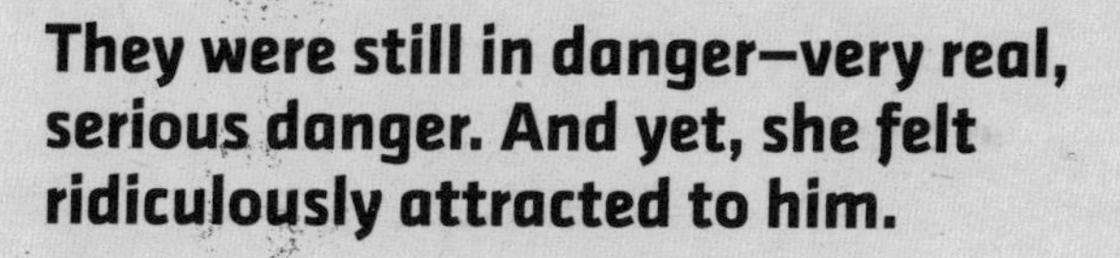

They were still in danger—very real, serious danger. And yet, she felt ridiculously attracted to him.

They'd both been hot, covered in swamp water, tinged with long grasses...

Her flesh was burned and scratched and raw...

And she was still breathing!

Was that it? She had survived. He had been a captor at first, and now he was a savior. Did all of this mess with the mind? Was she desperate to lean on the man because there was really something chemical and physical and real between them, or was she suffering some kind of mental break, brought on by all that had happened?

"Come on!" he urged her.

And they began to move again, deep into the swamp. She felt his hand on hers. And she felt a strange burning sensation...

Even as she shivered.

LAW AND DISORDER

New York Times and *USA TODAY* Bestselling Author

HEATHER GRAHAM

ISBN-13: 978-1-335-72077-1

Law and Disorder

This edition published by arrangement with Harlequin Books S.A.

For questions and comments about the quality of this book, please contact us at CustomerService@Harlequin.com.

Printed in U.S.A.

New York Times and *USA TODAY* bestselling author **Heather Graham** has written more than a hundred novels. She's a winner of the RWA's Lifetime Achievement Award and the International Thriller Writers' Silver Bullet. She is an active member of International Thriller Writers and Mystery Writers of America. For more information, check out her website: theoriginalheathergraham.com. You can also find Heather on Facebook.

Books by Heather Graham

Harlequin Intrigue

Law and Disorder

MIRA Books

Deadly Fate
Haunted Destiny
Flawless
The Hidden
The Forgotten
The Silenced

Visit the Author Profile page at Harlequin.com for more titles.

For Kathy Pickering, Traci Hall and Karen Kendall

Great and crazy road trips

Florida's MWA and FRA...

And my magnificent state, Florida

Chapter One

Dakota Cameron was stunned to turn and find a gun in her face. It was held by a tall, broad-shouldered man in a hoodie and a mask. The full-face rubber mask—like the Halloween "Tricky Dickie" masks of Richard Nixon—was familiar. It was a mask to denote a historic criminal, she thought, but which one?

The most ridiculous thing was that she almost giggled. She couldn't help but think back to when they were kids; all of them here, playing, imagining themselves notorious criminals. It had been the coolest thing in the world when her dad had inherited the old Crystal Manor on Crystal Island, off the Rickenbacker Causeway, between Miami and South Beach—despite the violence that was part of the estate's history, or maybe because of it.

She and her friends had been young, in grammar school at the time, and they'd loved the estate and all the rumors that had gone with it. They hadn't played cops and robbers—they had played cops and *gangsters*, calling each other G-Man or Leftie, or some other such silly name. Because her father was strict and there was no way crime would ever be glorified here—even if the place had once belonged to Anthony Green, one of the biggest mobsters to hit the causeway islands in the late 1940s and early 1950s—crime of any kind was seen as very, very bad. When the kids played games here, the coppers and the G-men always won.

Because of those old games, when Kody turned to find the gun in her face, she felt a smile twitching at her lips. But then the large man holding the gun fired over her head and the sign that bore the name Crystal Manor exploded into a million bits.

The gun-wielder was serious. It was not, as she had thought possible, a joke—not an old friend, someone who had heard she was back in Miami for the week, someone playing a prank.

No. No one she knew would play such a sick joke.

"Move!" a husky voice commanded her.

She was so stunned at the truth of the situation, the masked man staring at her, the bits of wood exploding around her, that she didn't give way to the weakness in her knees or the growing fear shooting through her. She simply responded.

"Move? To where? What do you want?"

"Out of the booth, up to the house, now. And fast!"

The "booth" was the old guardhouse that sat just inside the great wrought-iron gates on the road. It dated back to the early years of the 1900s when pioneer Jimmy Crystal had first decided upon the spit of high ground—a good three feet above the water level—to found his fishing camp. Coral rock had been dug out of nearby quarries for the foundations of what had then been the caretaker's cottage. Over the next decade, Jimmy Crystal's "fishing camp" had become a playground for the rich and famous. The grand house on the water had been built—pieces of it coming from decaying castles and palaces in Europe—the gardens had been planted and the dock had slowly extended out into Biscayne Bay.

In the 1930s, Jimmy Crystal had mysteriously disappeared at sea. The house and grounds had been swept up by the gangster Anthony Green. He had ruled there for years—until being brought down by a hail of bullets at his club on Miami Beach by "assailants unknown."

The Crystal family had come back in then. The last of them had died when Kody had been just six; that's when her father had discovered that Amelia Crystal—the last assumed member of the old family—had actually been his great-great-great-aunt.

Daniel Cameron had inherited the grandeur—and the ton of bills—that went with the estate.

"Now!" the gun wielder said.

Kody was amazed that her trembling legs could actually move.

"All right," she said, surprised by the even tone of her voice. "I'll have to open the door to get out. And, of course, you're aware that there are cameras all over this estate?"

"Don't worry about the cameras," he said.

She shrugged and moved from the open ticket window to the door. In the few feet between her and the heavy wooden door she tried to think of something she could do.

How in the hell could she sound the alarm?

Maybe it had already been sounded. Crystal Manor was far from the biggest tourist attraction in the area, but still, it *was* an attraction. The cops were aware of it. And Celestial Island—the bigger island that led to Crystal Island—was small, easily accessible by boat but, from the mainland, only accessible via the causeway and then the bridge. To reach Crystal Island, you needed to take the smaller bridge from Celestial Island—or, as with all the islands, arrive by boat. If help had been alerted, it might take time for it to get here.

Jose Marquez, their security man, often walked the walled area down to the water, around the back of the house and the lawn and the gardens and the maze, to the front. He was on his radio at all times. But, of course, with the gun in her face, she had no chance to call him.

Was Jose all right? she wondered. Had the gunman already gotten to him?

"What! Are you eighty? Move!"

The voice was oddly familiar. Was this an old friend? Had someone in her family even set this up, taunting her with a little bit of reproach for the decision she'd made to move up to New York City? She did love her home; leaving hadn't been easy. But she'd been offered a role in a "living theater" piece in an old hotel in the city, a part-time job at an old Irish pub through the acting friend who was part owner—and a rent-controlled apartment for the duration. She was home for a week—just a week—to set some affairs straight before final rehearsals and preview performances.

"Now! Get moving—now!" The man fired again and a large section of coral rock exploded.

Her mind began to race. She hadn't heard many good things about women who'd given in to knife- or gun-wielding strangers. They usually wound up dead anyway.

She ducked low, hurrying to the push button that would lower the aluminum shutter over the open window above the counter at the booth. Diving for her purse, she rolled away with it toward the stairway to the storage area above, dumping her purse as she did so. Her cell phone fell out and she grabbed for it.

But before she could reach it, there was another explosion. The gunman had shot through the lock on the heavy wooden door; it pushed inward.

He seemed to move with the speed of light. Her fingers had just closed around the phone when he straddled over her, wrenching the phone from her hand and throwing it across the small room. He hunkered down on his knees, looming large over her.

There wasn't a way that she was going to survive this! She thought, too, of the people up at the house, imagining distant days of grandeur, the staff, every one of which adored the house and the history. Thought of them all…with bullets in their heads.

With all she had she fought him, trying to buck him off her.

"For the love of God, stop," he whispered harshly, holding her down. "Do as I tell you. Now!"

"So you can kill me later?" she demanded, and stared up at him, trying not to shake. She was basically a coward and couldn't begin to imagine where any of her courage was coming from.

Instinctual desperation? The primal urge to survive?

Before he could answer there was a shout from behind him.

"Barrow! What the hell is going on in there?"

"We're good, Capone!" the man over her shouted back.

Capone?

"Cameras are all sizzled," the man called Capone called out. She couldn't see him. "Closed for Renovation signs up on the gates."

"Great. I've got this. You can get back to the house. We're good here. On the way now!"

"You're slower than molasses!" Capone barked. "Hurry the hell up! Dillinger and Floyd are securing the house."

Capone? As in "Al" Capone, who had made Miami his playground, along with Anthony Green? Dillinger—as in John Dillinger? Floyd—as in Pretty Boy Floyd?

Barrow—or the muscle-bound twit on top of her now—stared at her hard through the eye holes in his mask.

Barrow—as in Clyde Barrow. Yes, he was wearing a Clyde Barrow mask!

She couldn't help but grasp at hope. If they had all given themselves ridiculous 1930's gangster names and were wearing hoodies and masks, maybe cold-blooded murder might be avoided. These men may think their identities were well hidden and they wouldn't need to kill to avoid having any eye witnesses.

"Come with me!" Barrow said. She noted his eyes then. They were blue; an intense blue, almost navy.

Again something of recognition flickered within her. They were such unusual eyes…

"Come with me!"

She couldn't begin to imagine why she laughed, but she did.

"Wow, isn't that a movie line?" she asked. "*Terminator*! Good old Arnie Schwarzenegger. But aren't you supposed to say, 'Come with me—if you want to live'?"

He wasn't amused.

"Come with me—if you want to live," he said, emphasis on the last.

What was she supposed to do? He was a wall of a man, six-feet plus, shoulders like a linebacker.

"Then get off me," she snapped.

He moved, standing with easy agility, reaching a hand down to her.

She ignored the hand and rose on her own accord, heading for the shattered doorway. He quickly came to her side, still holding the gun but slipping an arm around her shoulders.

She started to shake him off.

"Dammit, do you want them to shoot you the second you step out?" He swore.

She gritted her teeth and allowed the touch until they were outside the guardhouse. Once they were in the clear, she shook him off.

"Now, I think you just have to point that gun at my back," she said, her voice hard and cold.

"Head to the main house," he told her.

The old tile path, cutting handsomely through the manicured front lawn of the estate, lay before her. It was nearing twilight and she couldn't help but notice that the air was perfect—neither too cold nor too hot—and that the setting sun was painting a palette of colors in the sky. She could smell the salt in the air and hear the waves as they splashed against the concrete breakers at the rear of the house.

All that made the area so beautiful—and, in particular, the house out on the island—had never seemed to be quite so evident and potent as when she walked toward the house. Jimmy Crystal had not actually named the place for himself; he'd written in his old journal that the island had seemed to sit in a sea of crystals, shimmering beneath the sun. And so it was. And now, through the years, the estate had become something glimmering and dazzling, as well. It sat in homage to days gone by, to memories of a time when the international city of Miami had been little more than a mosquito-ridden swamp and only those with vision had seen what might come in the future.

She and her parents had never lived in the house; they'd stayed in their home in the Roads section of the city, just north of Coconut Grove, where they'd always lived. They managed the estate, but even in that, a board had been brought in and a trust set up. The expenses to keep such an estate going were staggering.

While it had begun as a simple fishing shack, time

and the additions of several generations had made Crystal Manor into something much more. It resembled both an Italianate palace and a medieval castle with tile and marble everywhere, grand columns, turrets and more. The manor was literally a square built around a center courtyard, with turrets at each corner that afforded four tower rooms above the regular two stories of the structure.

As she walked toward the sweeping, grand steps that led to the entry, she looked around. She had heard one of the other thugs, but, at that moment, she didn't see anyone.

Glancing back, she saw that a chain had been looped around the main gate. The gate arched to fifteen feet; the coral rock wall that surrounded the house to the water was a good twelve feet. Certainly not insurmountable by the right law-enforcement troops, but, still, a barrier against those who might come in to save the day.

She looked back at her masked abductor. She could see nothing of his face—except for those eyes.

Why were they so…eerily familiar? If she really knew him, if she had known him growing up, she'd have remembered who went with those eyes! They were striking, intense. The darkest, deepest blue she had ever seen.

What was she thinking? He was a crook! She didn't make friends with crooks!

The double entryway doors suddenly opened and she saw another man in its maw.

Kody stopped. She stared at the doors. They were

really beautiful, hardwood enhanced with stained-glass images of pineapples—symbols of welcome. Quite ironic at the moment.

"Get her in here!" the second masked man told the one called Barrow.

"Go," Barrow said softly from behind her.

She walked up the steps and into the entry.

It was grand now, though the entry itself had once been the whole house built by Jimmy Crystal when he had first fallen in love with the little island that, back then, had been untouched, isolated—a haven only for mangroves and mosquitos. Since then, of course, the island—along with Star and Hibiscus islands—had become prime property.

But the foyer still contained vestiges of the original. The floor was coral rock. The columns were the original columns that Jimmy Crystal had poured. Dade country pine still graced the side walls.

The rear wall had been taken down to allow for glass barriers to the courtyard; more columns had been added. The foyer contained only an 1890's rocking horse to the right side of the double doors and an elegant, old fortune-telling machine to the left. And, of course, the masked man who stood between the majestic staircases that led to the second floor at each side of the space.

She cast her eyes around but saw no one else.

There had still been four or five guests on the property when Kody had started to close down for the day. And five staff members: Stacey Carlson, the estate manager, Nan Masters, his assistant, and Vince Jenkins, Brandi Johnson and Betsy Rodriguez, guides. Manny Diaz, the caretaker, had been off the property all day. And, of course, Jose Marquez was there somewhere.

"So, this is Miss Cameron?" the masked man in the house asked.

"Yes, Dillinger. This is Miss Cameron," Barrow said.

Dillinger. She was right—this guy's mask was that of the long-ago killer John Dillinger.

"Well, well, well. I can't tell you, Miss Cameron, what a delight it is to meet you!" the man said. "Imagine! When I heard that you were here—cuddle time with the family before the final big move to the Big Apple—I knew it was time we had to step in."

The man seemed to know about her—and her family.

"If you think I'm worth some kind of ransom," she said, truly puzzled—and hoping she wasn't sealing her own doom, "I'm not. We may own this estate, but it's in some kind of agreement and trust with the state of Florida. It survives off of grants and tourist dollars." She hesitated. "My family isn't rich. They just love this old place."

"Yeah, yeah, yeah, Daddy is an archeologist and Mom travels with him. Right now they're on their way back from South America so they can head up north with their baby girl to get her all settled into New York City. Yes! I have the prize right here, don't I?"

"I have no idea what you're talking about," Kody told him. "I wish I could say that someone would give you trillions of dollars for me, but I'm not anyone's prize. I'm a bartender-waitress at an Irish pub who's struggling to make ends meet as an actress."

"Oh, honey," Dillinger said, "I don't give a damn if you're a bad actress."

"Hey! I never said I was a *bad* actress!" she protested. And then, of course, she thought that he was making her crazy—heck, the whole situation was making her crazy—because who the hell cared if she was a bad actress or a good actress if she wasn't even alive?

Dillinger waved a hand in the air. "That's neither here nor there. You're going to lead us to the Anthony Green stash."

Startled, Kody went silent.

Everyone, of course, had heard about the Anthony Green *stash.*

Green was known to have knocked over the long-defunct Miami Bank of the Pioneers, making off with the bank's safe-deposit boxes that had supposedly contained millions in diamonds, jewels, gold and more. It was worth millions. But Anthony Green had died in a hail of bullets—with his mouth shut. The stash was never found. It had always been suspected that Anthony Green—before his demise—had seen to it that the haul had been hidden somewhere in one of his shacks deep in the Everglades, miles from his Biscayne Bay home.

Rumor followed rumor. It was said that Guillermo Salazar—a South American drug lord—had actually found the stash about a decade ago and added a small fortune in ill-gotten heroin-sales gains to it—before he, in turn, had been shot down by a rival drug cartel.

Who the hell knew? One way or the other, it was supposedly a very large fortune.

She didn't doubt that Salazar had sold drugs; the Coast Guard in South Florida was always busy stopping the drug trade. But she sure as hell didn't believe that Salazar had found the Green stash at the house, because she really didn't believe the stash was here.

Chills suddenly rose up her spine.

If she was supposed to find a stash that didn't exist here...

They were all dead.

"Where is everyone?" she asked.

"Safe," Dillinger said.

"Safe where?"

No one answered Kody. "Where?" she repeated.

"They're all fine, Miss Cameron."

It was the man behind her—Barrow—who finally spoke up. "Dillinger, she needs to know that they're all fine," he added.

"I assure you," Dillinger continued. "They're all fine. They're in the music room."

The music room took up most of the left side of the downstairs. It would be the right place to hold a group of people.

Except...

Someone, somewhere, had to know that something was going on here. Surely one of the employees or guests had had a chance to get out a cell phone warning.

"I want to see them," she said. "I want to see that everyone is all right."

"Listen, missy, what you do and don't want doesn't matter here. What you're going to do for us matters," Dillinger told her.

"I don't know where the stash is. If I did, the world would have known about it long ago," she said. "And, if you know everything, you surely know that history says Anthony Green hid his bank treasure in some hut somewhere out in the Everglades."

"She sure as hell isn't rich, Dillinger," Barrow said. "Everything is true—she's taken a part-time job because what she's working is off-off Broadway. If she knew about the stash, I don't think she'd be slow-pouring Guinness at an old pub in the city."

Dillinger seemed annoyed. Kody was, in fact, surprised by what she could read in his eyes—and in his movements.

"No one asked your opinion, Barrow," Dillinger said. "She's the only one who can find it. I went through every newspaper clipping—she's loved the place since she was a kid. She's read everything on Jimmy Crystal and Anthony Green and the mob days on Miami Beach. She knows what rooms in this place were built what years, when any restoration was done. She knows it all. She knows how to find the stash. And she's going to help us find it."

"Don't be foolish," Kody said. "You can get out now. No one knows who you guys are—the masks, I'll grant you, are good. Well, they're not good. They're cheap and lousy masks, but they create the effect you want and no one here knows what your real faces look like. Pretty soon, though, walls or not, cops will swarm the place. Someone will come snooping around. Someone probably got something out on a cell phone."

She couldn't see his face but she knew that Dillinger smiled. "Cell phones? No, we secured those pretty quickly," he said. "And your security guard? He's resting—he's got a bit of a headache." He shook his head. "Face it, young lady. You have me and Barrow here. Floyd is with your friends, Capone is on his way to help, and the overall estate is being guarded by Baby Face Nelson and Machine Gun Kelly and our concept of modern security and communication and, you know, we've got good old Dutch—as in Schultz—working it all, too. I think we're good for a while. Long enough for you to figure out where the stash is. And, let's see, you are going to help us."

"I won't do anything," she told him. "Nothing. Nothing at all—not until I know that my friends and our guests are safe and that Jose isn't suffering from anything more than a headache."

Not that she'd help them even then—if she even could. The stash had been missing since the 1930s. In fact, Anthony Green had used a similar ruse when he had committed the bank robbery. He'd come in fast with six men—all wearing masks. He'd gotten out just as fast. The cops had never gotten him. They'd suspected him, but they'd never had proof. They'd still been trying to find witnesses and build a case against him when he'd been gunned down on Miami Beach.

But her demands must have hit home because Dillinger turned to Barrow. "Fine. Bring her through."

He turned to head down the hallway that led into

the music room—the first large room on the left side of the house.

It was a gorgeous room, graced with exquisite crown molding, rich burgundy carpets and old seascapes of famous ports, all painted by various masters in colors that complemented the carpet. There was a wooden dais at one end of the room that accommodated a grand piano, a harp, music stands and room for another three or four musicians.

There were sofas, chairs and love seats backed to all the walls, and a massive marble fireplace for those times when it did actually get cold on the water.

Kody knew about every piece in the room, but at that moment all she saw was the group huddled together on the floor.

Quickly searching the crowd, she found Stacey Carlson, the estate manager. He was sixty or so with salt-and-pepper hair, old-fashioned sideburns and a small mustache and goatee. A dignified older man, he was quick to smile, slow to follow a joke—but brilliant. Nan Masters was huddled to his side. If it was possible to have platonic affairs, the two of them were hot and heavy. Nothing ever went on beyond their love of Miami, the beaches and all that made up their home. Nan was red-haired, but not in the least fiery. Slim and tiny, she looked like a cornered mouse huddled next to Stacey.

Vince Jenkins sat cross-legged on a Persian rug that lay over the carpet, straight and angry. There was a bruise forming on the side of his face. He'd apparently started out by fighting back.

Beside him, Betsy Rodriguez and Brandi Johnson were close to one another. Betsy, the tinier of the two, but by far the most out-there and sarcastic, had her arm around Brandi, who was nearly six feet, blond, blue-eyed, beautiful and shy.

Jose Marquez had been laid on the largest love seat. His forehead was bleeding, but, Kody quickly saw, he was breathing.

The staff had been somewhat separated from the few guests who had remained on the property, finishing up in the gardens after closing. She couldn't remember all their names but she recalled the couple, Victor and Melissa Arden. They were on their honeymoon, yet they'd just been in Texas, visiting the graves of Bonnie Parker and Clyde Barrow in their separate cemeteries. They loved studying old gangsters, which was beyond ironic, Kody thought now. Another young woman from Indiana, an older man and a fellow of about forty rounded out the group.

They were all huddled low, apparently respecting the twin guns carried by another man in an identity-concealing mask.

"Kody!" Stacey said, breathing out a sigh of relief. She realized that her friends might have been worrying for her life.

She turned to Dillinger. "You'd better not hurt them!"

"Hurt them?" Dillinger said. "I don't want to hurt any of you, really. Okay, okay, so, quite frankly, I don't give a rat's ass. But Barrow there, he's kind of squeamish when it comes to blood and guts. Capone—my friend with the guns—is kind of rabid. Like he really had syphilis or rabies or something. He'd just as soon shoot you as look at you. So, here's my suggestion." He paused, staring Cody up and down. "You find out what I need to know. You come up to that library—and you start using everything you know and going through everything in the books, every news brief, every everything. You find that stash for me. Their lives depend on it."

"What if I can't find it?" she asked. "No one has found this stash in eighty-plus years!"

"You'd better find it," Dillinger said.

"Help will come!" Betsy said defiantly. "This is crazy—you're crazy! SWAT teams aren't but a few miles away. Someone—"

"You'd better hope no one comes," Dillinger said. He walked over to hunker down in front of her. "Because that's the whole point of hostages. They want you to live. They probably don't give a rat's ass one way or the other, either, but that's what they're paid to do. Get the hostages out alive. But, to prove we mean business, we'll have to start by killing someone and tossing out the body. And guess what? We like to start with the big-mouths, the wise-asses!"

He reached out to Betsy and that was all the impetus Kody needed. She sure as hell wasn't particularly courageous but she didn't waste a second to think. She just bolted toward Dillinger, smashing into him with such force that he went flying down.

With her.

He was strong, really strong.

He was up in two seconds, dragging her up with him.

"Why you little bitch!" he exclaimed as he hauled his arm back, ready to slam a jaw-breaking fist into her face.

His hand never reached her.

Barrow—with swift speed and agility—was on the two of them. She felt a moment of pain as he wrenched her out of Dillinger's grasp, thrusting himself between them.

"No, Dillinger, no. Keep the hostages in good shape. This one especially! We need her, Dillinger. We need her!"

"Bitch! You saw her—she tackled me."

"We need her!"

The hostages had started to move, scrambling back, restless, frightened, and Capone shoved someone with the butt of his gun.

Barrow lifted his gun and shot the ceiling.

Plaster fell around them all like rain.

And the room went silent.

"Let's get her out of here and up to the library, Dillinger. Dammit, now. Come on—let's do what we came here to do!" he insisted. "I'm into money—not a body count."

Kody felt his hand as he gripped her arm, ready to drag her along.

Dillinger stared at him a long moment.

Was there a struggle going on? she wondered. A power play? Dillinger seemed to be the boss, but then Barrow had stepped in. He'd saved her from a good beating, at the least. She couldn't help but feel that there was something better about him.

She was even drawn to him.

Oh, that was sick, she told herself. He was a crook, maybe even a killer.

Still, he didn't seem to be as bloodthirsty as Dillinger.

Dillinger stepped around her and Barrow, heading for the stairs to the library. Barrow followed with her.

"Hey!"

They heard the call when they had nearly cleared the room.

She turned to see Capone standing next to Betsy Rodriguez. He wasn't touching her; he was just close to her.

He moved his gun, running the muzzle through her hair.

"Dakota Cameron!" he said. "The world—well, your world—is dependent on your every thought and word!"

She started to move toward him but Barrow stopped her, whispering in her ear, "Don't get them going!"

She couldn't help herself. She called out to Capone. "You're here because you want something? Well, if you want it from me, step the hell away from my friend!"

To her surprise, Dillinger started to laugh.

"We've got a wild card on our hands, for sure. Come on, Capone. Let's accommodate the lady. Step away from her friend."

From behind her, Barrow added, "Come on, Capone. I'm in this for the money and a quick trip out of the country. Let's get her started working and get this the hell done, huh? Beat her to pieces or put a bullet in her, and she's worthless."

"Miss Cameron?" Dillinger said, sweeping an elegant bow to her. "My men will behave like gentlemen—as long as your friends let them. You hear that, right?"

"I can be a perfect gentleman!" Capone called back to him.

"Tell them all to sit tight and not make trouble—that you will manage to get what we want," Barrow said to her.

She looked at him again.

Those eyes of his! So deep, dark, blue and intense!

Surely, if she really knew him, she'd recognize him now.

She didn't. Still, she couldn't help but feel that she did, and that the man she knew wasn't a criminal, and that she had been drawn to those eyes before.

She shivered suddenly, looking at him.

He didn't like blood and guts—that's what Dillinger had said.

Maybe he was a thief, a hood—but hated the idea of being a murderer. Maybe, just maybe, he did want to keep them all alive.

"Hey!" she called back to the huddled group of captives. "I know everything about the house and all about Anthony Green and the gangster days. Just hold tight and be cool, please. I can do this. I know I can do this!"

They all looked at her with hope in their faces.

She gazed at Barrow and said, "They need water. We keep cases of water bottles in the lower cabinet of the kitchen. Go through the music room and the dining room and you'll reach the kitchen. I would truly appreciate if you would give them all water. It will help me think."

But it was Dillinger who replied.

"Sure," he said. "You think—and we'll just be the nicest group of guys you've ever met!"

Chapter Two

Nick Connolly—known as Barrow to the Coconut Grove crew of murderers, thieves and drug runners who were careful not to share their real names, even with one another—was doing his best. His damned best.

Which wasn't easy.

Nick didn't mind undercover work. He could even look away from the drugs and the prostitution, knowing that what he was doing would stop the flow of some really bad stuff onto the city streets—and put away some really bad men.

From the moment he'd infiltrated this gang three weeks ago, the situation had been crazy, but he'd also thought it would work. This would be the time when he could either get them all together in an escape boat that the Coast Guard would be ready to swoop up, or, if that kind of maneuver failed, pick them off one by one. Each of these guys—Dillinger, Capone, Floyd, Nelson, Kelly and Schultz—had killed or committed some kind of an armed robbery. They were all ex-cons. Capone had been the one to believe in Nick's off-color stories in an old dive bar in Coconut Grove, and as far as Capone knew, Nick had been locked up in Leavenworth, convicted of a number of crimes. Of course, Capone had met Nick as Ted—Ted Johnson had been the pseudonym Nick had been using in South Florida. There really had been a Ted Johnson; he'd died in the prison hospital ward of a knife wound. But no one knew that. No one except certain members of the FBI and the hospital staff and warden and other higher ups at the prison.

None of these men—especially "Dillinger"—had any idea that Nick had full dossiers on them. As far as they all knew, they were anonymous, even with each other.

Undercover was always tricky.

It should have been over today; he should have been able to give up the undercover work and head back to New York City. Not that he minded winter in Miami.

He just hated the men with whom he had now aligned himself—even if it was to bring them down, and even if it was important work.

Today should have been it.

But all the plans he'd discussed with his local liaisons and with Craig Frasier—part of the task force from New York that had been chasing the drug-and-murder-trail of the man called Dillinger from New York City down through the South—had gone to hell.

And the stakes had risen like a rocket—because of a situation he'd just found out about that morning.

Without the aid, knowledge or consent of the others, for added protection, Dillinger had kidnapped a boy right before they had all met to begin their take-over of the Crystal Estate.

It wouldn't have mattered who the kid was to Nick—he'd have done everything humanly possible to save him—but the kidnapped boy was the child of Holden Burke, mayor of South Beach. Dillinger had assured them all that he had the kid safely hidden somewhere—where, exactly, he wasn't telling any of them. They all knew that people could talk, so it was safer that only he knew the whereabouts of little Adrian Burke. And not to worry—the kid was alive. He was their pass-go ace in the hole.

That was one thing.

Then, there was Dakota Cameron.

To be fair, Nick didn't exactly know Kody Cameron but he had seen her—and she had seen him—in New York City.

And the one time that he'd seen her, he'd known immediately that he'd wanted to see her again.

And now, here they were. In a thousand years he'd never imagined their second meeting would be like this.

No one had known that Dillinger's game plan ended with speculation—the vague concept that he could kidnap Dakota, take her prisoner—and *hope* she could find the stash!

Dillinger planned the heists and the drug runs; he worked with a field of prostitution that included the pimps and the girls. He had South American contacts. No one had figured he'd plan on taking over the old Crystal Estate, certain that he could find a Cameron family member who knew where to find the old mob treasure.

So, now, here he was—surprised and somewhat anxious to realize that the lovely young brunette with the fascinating eyes he'd brushed by at Finnegan's on Broadway in New York City would show up at the ticket booth at a Florida estate and tourist attraction.

Craig Frasier, one of the main men on the task force Director Egan had formed to trace and track "Dillinger," aka Nathan Appleby, along the Eastern seaboard, spent a lot of time at Finnegan's. The new love of his life was co-owner, along with her brothers, of the hundred-and-fifty-year-old pub in downtown Manhattan.

Nick and Kody Cameron had passed briefly, like proverbial ships in the night, but he hadn't had the least problem recognizing her today. He knew her, because they had both paused to stare at one another at the pub.

Instant attraction? Definitely on his part and he could have sworn on hers, too.

Then she'd muttered some kind of swift apology and Craig's new girlfriend, who'd come over to greet them, explained, "That's Kody Cameron. She's working a living theater piece with my brother. Sounds kind of cool, right? And she's working here part-time now, making the transition to New York."

"What's living theater?" Nick had asked Kieran Finnegan.

"Kevin could tell you better than me," she had explained, "but it's taking a show more as a concept than as a structured piece and working with the lines loosely while interacting with the audience as your character."

Whatever she did, he'd hoped that he'd see her again; he'd even figured that he could. While Kieran Finnegan actually worked as a psychologist and therapist for a pair of psychiatrists who often came in as consultants for the New York office of the Bureau, she was also often at Finnegan's. And since he was working tightly with Craig and his partner, Mike, and a cyber-force on this case, he'd figured he'd be back in Finnegan's, too. But then, of course, Dillinger had come south, met up with old prison mates Capone, Nelson, Kelly, Floyd and Schultz, and Nick—who had gone through high school in South Florida and still had family in the area—had been sent down to infiltrate the gang.

The rest, as the saying went, was history.

Now, if Dakota Cameron saw his face, if she gave any indication that she knew him, and knew that he was an FBI man…

They'd both be dead.

And it didn't help the situation that she was battle ready—ready to lay down her life for her friends.

Then again, there should have been a way for him to stop this. If it hadn't been for the little boy who had been taken…

He had to find out where the kid was. Had Dillinger stashed him with friends or associates? Had he hidden him somewhere? It wasn't as hard to hide somewhere here as one would think, with the land being just about at sea level and flat as a pancake. There were enough crack houses and abandoned tenements. Of course, Nick was pretty sure Dillinger couldn't have snatched the kid at a bus station, hidden him wherever, and made it to the estate at their appointed time, if he had gone far.

But that knowledge didn't help much.

Nick's first case when he'd started with the Bureau in the Miami offices had been finding the truth behind the bodies stuffed in barrels, covered with acid and tossed in the Everglades.

He refused to think of that image along with his fear for the child; the boy was alive. Adrian Burke wouldn't be worth anything in an escape situation if he was dead.

Nick wiped away that thought and leaned against the door frame as he stood guard over Kody. Capone was now just on the other side of the door.

Like the entire estate, the library was kept in pristine shape, but it also held an air of fading and decaying elegance, making one feel a sense of nostalgia. The floors were marble, covered here and there by Persian throw rugs, and built-in bookshelves were filled with volumes that appeared older than the estate itself, along with sea charts and more.

Kody Cameron had a ledger opened before her, but she was looking at him. Quizzically.

It seemed as if she suspected she knew him but couldn't figure out from where.

"You're not as crazy as the others," she said softly. "I can sense that about you. But you need to do something to stop this. That treasure he's talking about has been missing for years and years. God knows, maybe it's in the Everglades, swallowed up in a sinkhole. You don't want to be a part of this—I know you don't. And those guys are lethal. They'll hurt someone…kill someone. This is still a death penalty state, you know. Please, if you would just—"

He found himself walking over to her at the desk and replying in a heated whisper, "Just do what he says and find the damned treasure. Lie if you have to! Find something that will make Dillinger believe that you know where the treasure is. Give him a damned map to find it. He won't think twice about killing people, but he won't kill just for the hell of it. Don't give him a reason."

"You're not one of them. You have to stop this. Get away from them," she said.

She was beautiful, earnest, passionate. He wanted to reassure her. To rip off his mask and tell her that law enforcement was on it all.

But that was impossible, lest they all die quickly.

He had to keep his distance and keep her, the kidnapped child and the others in the house alive.

Capone was growing curious. He left his post at the archway and walked in. "Hey. What's going on here? Don't interrupt the woman, Barrow. I want to get the hell out of here! I've done some wild things with Dillinger, but this is taking the cake. Makes me more nervous than twenty cartel members in a gunboat. Leave her be."

"Yeah. I'm going to leave her be. And she's going to come up with something," Barrow said.

He'd barely spoken when Schultz came rushing in.

While Capone knew how to rig a central box and stop cameras and security systems, Schultz was an expert sharpshooter. He was tall and thin, not much in the muscles department, but Nick had seen him take long shots that were just about impossible.

"News is out that we're here," he said. "Cops are surrounding the gates. I fired a few warning shots and Dillinger answered the phone—told them we have a pack of hostages. You should see them all out there at the gates," he added, his grin evident in his voice. "They look like a pack of chickens. Guess they're calling for a hostage negotiator. Dillinger is deciding whether to give them a live one or a body."

Kody Cameron stood. "They give him a body and I'm done. If he gives them one body, it won't make any difference to him if he kills the rest of us."

"And just how far are you getting, sweet thing?" Schultz asked, coming close to her. He reached out to lift the young woman's chin.

Nick struggled to control himself. Hell, she wasn't just a captive. Not just someone he had to keep alive.

She worked for Finnegan's. She was connected to Kevin Finnegan and Kieran Finnegan—and therefore, to Craig Frasier.

And he noticed her the first time he'd ever seen her. Known that he'd wanted to see her again.

He'd never imagined it could be in this way.

For a moment he managed to keep his peace. But, damn her, she just had to react. Schultz cradled her face and she stepped back and pushed his hand away.

"Hey, hey, hey, little girl. You don't want to get hurt, do you? Be nice."

Nick stepped up, swinging Schultz around.

"Leave her alone, dammit. We're here for a reason."

"What? Are you sweet on her yourself?" Schultz asked him, his tone edgy. "You think this is merchandise you keep all for yourself?"

"I'm not merchandise!" Kody snapped.

"I want her to find what Dillinger wants, and I want to get the hell out of here!" Nick said. He was as tall as Schultz; he had a lot more muscle and he was well trained. In a fair fight, Schultz wouldn't stand a chance against him.

There were no fair fights here, he reminded himself. He had to keep an even keel.

"Leave her alone and let her get back to work," he said. "Get your mind on the job to be done here."

"Shouldn't you be up in one of the front towers?" Capone asked Schultz. "Isn't that your job in all this?"

Schultz gave them all a sweeping and withering glare. Then he turned and left.

Capone was staring at Nick. "Maybe you should get your mind on the job, too, Barrow," he suggested.

"And you," Nick added softly.

Capone continued to stare at him.

It went no further as Dillinger came striding into the room. He ignored Capone and Nick and walked straight to the desk and Kody.

"How long?" he asked her.

"How long? You're asking me to do something no one has managed in decades," Kody said.

"You're got two hours," Dillinger said. "Two hours. They're bringing in a hostage negotiator. Don't make me prove that I will kill."

"I'm doing my best," Kody said.

"Where's the phone in this room?" Dillinger asked.

"On the table by the door, next to the Tiffany lamp," Kody said.

"What the hell is a Tiffany lamp?" Dillinger demanded, leaning in on Kody.

"There. Right there, boss," Nick said, pointing out the elegant little side table with the lamp and the white trim-line phone. He walked over to it and saw that the volume was off.

"Ready for calls," he told Dillinger.

"Good. We'll manage it from here. Capone, get on down and help Nelson with the hostages. Schultz is in the eagle's seat in the right tower. Floyd's in the left. And we've got our good old boy, our very own private Machine Gun Kelly, in the back. Don't trust those hostages, though. I'm thinking if we have to get rid of a few, we'll be in better shape."

"No, we won't be," Nick said flatly. "You hurt a hostage, it tells the cops that they're not doing any good with negotiation. We have to keep them believing they're getting everyone back okay. That's the reason they'll hold off. If they think we're just going to kill people, they'll storm us, figuring to kill us before we kill the hostages. That's the logic they teach, trust me," Nick told Dillinger.

Dillinger shrugged, looking at the phone. "Well,

we'll give them a little time, if nothing else. So, Miss Cameron, just how are you doing?"

Dakota Cameron looked up and stared at Dillinger, then cocked her head at an angle. "Looking for a needle in a haystack?" she asked. "I'm moving some hay out of the way, but there's still a great deal to go. You do realize—"

"Yes, yes," Dillinger said impatiently. "Yes, everyone has looked for years. But not because their lives were at stake. You're holding so many precious souls in your hands, Miss Cameron. I'm just so sure that will help you follow every tiny lead to just where the treasure can be found."

"Well, I'll try to keep a clear head here," she said. "At the moment, my mind is not hampered with grief over losing anyone, and you really should keep it that way. I mean, if you want me to find out anything for you."

Nick wished he could have shut her up somehow; he couldn't believe she was taunting a man who was half-crazy and holding the lives of so many people in his hands.

He had to admire her bravado—even as he wished she didn't have it.

But Dillinger laughed softly beneath his mask.

"My dear Miss Cameron, you do have more balls than half the men I find myself working with!" Dillinger told her. "Excellent—if you have results. If you don't, well, it will just make it all the easier to shut you up!"

She wasn't even looking at Dillinger anymore. She'd

turned her attention back to the journal spread open before her.

"Let me work," she said softly.

Dillinger grunted. He took a seat in one of the chairs by the wall of the library, near the phone.

Nick walked to the windows, looking out at the gardens in the front of the house, the driveway and—at a distance—the wall and the great iron gates that led up to the house.

More and more cars were beginning to arrive—marked police cars, unmarked cars belonging to the FBI and other law-enforcement agencies.

He wondered how Dillinger could believe he might get out of this alive.

And then he wondered just how the hell any of them were going to get out alive.

The phone began to ring. Dakota Cameron jumped in her chair, nearly leaping from it.

Nick nearly jumped himself.

Dillinger rose and picked up the phone. "Hello? Dillinger here. How can I help you? Other than keeping the hostages alive… Let's see, how can you help me? Well, I'll begin to explain. Right now, everyone in the house is breathing. We have some employees, we have some guests… What we want is more time, really good speed boats—cigarettes or Donzis will do. Now, of course, we need a couple because a few of these good people will be going with us for just a bit when we leave. We'll see to it that you get them all back alive and well as long as we get what we want."

Nick wished he was on an extension. He wanted to hear what was being said.

He saw Dillinger nod. "How bright of you to ask so quickly! Yes, there is a missing child, too, isn't there? An important little boy—son of a mayor! Ah, well, all children are important, aren't they…? Mr. Frasier? Ah! Sorry, Special Agent Frasier. FBI. They've brought in the big guns. Let's go with this—right now, I want time. You give me some time and you arrange for those boats. To be honest, I'm working on a way to give you back that kid I scooped up. Not a bad kid, in the least. I liked him. I'd hate for him to die of neglect, caged and chained and forgotten. So, you work on those boats."

Nick saw Dakota Cameron frown as she'd heard the name Frasier. Not that Frasier was a rare name, but Kody was good friends with Kevin Finnegan and therefore friends with his sister Kieran—and so she knew Craig. She had to be puzzled, wondering first if he was indeed the same man a friend was dating and, if so, what he was doing in South Florida.

She looked up from her ledger. She was staring at Dillinger hard, brows knit in a frown.

A moment later Dillinger set the receiver back in the cradle. He seemed to be pleased with himself.

"You kidnapped a child?" she asked.

"I like to have a backup plan," Dillinger said.

"You have all of us."

"Yes. But, hey, maybe nobody cares about any of you. They will care about a kid."

"Yep, they will," Nick interrupted. "But I think they need to believe in us, too. Hey, man, you want time for

Miss Cameron to find the treasure, the stash, or whatever might be hidden? If we're going to buy that time, we need to play to them. I say we give them the security guard. He needs medical attention. Best we get him out of here. An injured hostage is just a liability. Let's give him up as a measure of good faith."

"Maybe," Dillinger said. He looked at Kody. "How are you doing?"

"I'd do a lot better if you didn't ask me every other minute," she said. "And," she added softly, "if I wasn't so worried about Jose."

"Who the hell is Jose?" Dillinger asked.

"Our security guard. The injured man," Kody said.

Dillinger glanced restlessly at his watch and then at the phone. "Give them a few minutes to get back to me."

He walked out of the room, leaving Nick alone with Kody.

"How *are* you doing?" he asked her.

She shrugged and then looked up at him. "So far, I have all the same information everyone has had for years. Anthony Green robbed the bank, but the police couldn't pin it on him, couldn't make an arrest. He wrote in his own journal that it was great watching them all run around like chickens with no heads. Of course, it wouldn't be easy for anyone to find the stash. What it seems to me—from what I've read—is that he did plan on disappearing. Leaving the country. And he was talking about boats, as well—"

She broke off, staring at the old journal she was reading and then flipping pages over.

"What is it?" Nick asked.

She looked up at him, her expression suddenly guarded. He realized that—to her—he was a death-dealing criminal.

"I'm not sure," she said. "I need time."

"You've got time right now. Use it," he said.

"We need to see some of the hostages out of here—returned to safety," she said firmly. "In good faith!"

They were both startled by the sound of a gunshot. Then a barrage of bullets seemed to come hailing down on the house.

A priceless vase on a table exploded.

Nick practically flew across the room, leaping over the desk to land on top of Kody—and bring her down to the floor.

The barrage of bullets continued for a moment—and then went silent.

He felt her move beneath him.

He looked down at her. Her eyes were wide on his as she studied him gravely. He hadn't just been intrigued, he realized. He hadn't just wanted to see her again.

He'd been attracted to her. Really attracted.

And now…

She was trembling slightly.

He leaped to his feet, drawing her up, pulling her along with him as he raced down the hall to the stairs that led to the right tower where Schultz had been keeping guard.

Nick was pretty damned certain Schultz—a man who was crazy and more than a little trigger happy—had fired the first shots.

“What the hell are you doing?” he shouted.

As he did so, Dillinger came rushing along, as well. “What the hell?” he demanded furiously.

“I saw ’em moving, boss. I saw ’em moving!” Schultz shouted down.

The phone started ringing. Nick looked at Dillinger. “Let me take it. Let me see what I can do,” he said.

Dillinger was already moving back toward the library. Nick followed, still clasping Kody’s hand.

When they reached the library, Dillinger stepped back and let Nick answer the phone.

“Hello?” Nick said. “This is Barrow speaking now. We don’t know what happened. We do know that you responded with the kind of violence that’s going to get someone killed. Seriously, do you want everyone in here dead? What the hell was that?”

“Shots were fired at us,” a voice said. “Who is this?”

“I told you. Barrow.”

“Are you the head man?”

Nick glanced over at Dillinger.

“No. I’m spokesman for the head man. He’s all into negotiation. What we want doesn’t have anything to do with a bunch of dead men and women, but that’s what we could wind up with if we don’t get this going right,” Nick said.

“We don’t want dead people,” the voice on the other end assured him.

“We don’t, either,” Nick said.

“Barrow. All right, let’s talk. I think everyone got a little panicky. No one wants anyone to die here today.

We're all working in the same direction, that being to see that everyone gets out alive. Okay?"

Nick knew who was doing the negotiating for the array of cops and FBI and law enforcement just on the other side of the gates.

He was speaking with Craig Frasier. Nick was glad the FBI and the local authorities had gotten it together to make the situation go smoothly. He knew Craig; Craig knew him. There was so much more he was going to be able to do with Craig at the other end.

"How are they doing on my boats?" Dillinger asked, staring at Nick.

"We're going to need those boats," Nick said. He needed to give Craig all the information he could about the situation, without making Dillinger suspicious, and he wanted, also, to maintain his position as spokesman for Dillinger.

"Yes, two boats, right?" Craig asked.

"Good ones. The best speedboats you can get your hands on. Now, we're not fools. You won't get all the information you need to save everyone until we're long gone and safe. But, right now, we're going to give you a man. Security guard. He's got a bit of a gash on his head. We're going to bring him out to the front and we'll see that the gate is opened long enough for one of you to get him out. Do you understand? The fate of everyone here may depend on this nice gesture on our part going well."

He knew that Craig understood; Nick had really just told him the guard had been the only one injured and that he did need help.

“No one else is hurt? Everyone is fine?”

Craig had to ask to keep their cover. But Nick knew the agent was also concerned for Dakota Cameron. That the Cameron family owned this place—and that Kody was down here—was something Craig must have realized from the moment Dillinger made his move.

“No one is hurt. I’m trying to keep it that way,” Nick assured him, glancing over at Dillinger.

Dillinger nodded. He seemed to approve of how Nick handled the negotiations. There was enough of a low-lying threat in Nick’s tone to make it all sound very menacing, no matter what the words.

“That’s good. Open the gate and we’ll get the man. There will be no attempts to break in on you, no more bullets fired,” Craig said.

Nick looked at Dillinger. *Yes?* he mouthed.

Dillinger nodded. “Keep an eye on her!”

As he hurried out, Kody stood and started after him, then paused herself, as if certain Nick would have stopped her if she hadn’t. He held the phone and stared at her, wishing he dared tell her who he was and what his part was in all this.

But he couldn’t.

He couldn’t risk her betraying him.

He covered the mouthpiece on the house phone. “Don’t leave the room.”

“Jose Marquez…” she murmured.

“He’s really letting him go,” Nick said.

She walked over to him suddenly. He was afraid she was going to reach for the mask that covered his face.

She didn’t touch him. Instead she spoke quickly.

"You're not like that. You could stop this. You have a gun. You could—"

"Shoot them all down?" he asked her.

"Wound them, stop this—stop them from killing innocent people. I'd speak for you. I'd see that everyone in court knew that people survived because of you."

She was moving closer as she spoke—not to touch him, he realized, but to take his gun.

He set the phone down and grabbed her roughly by the wrists.

"Don't pull this on anyone else. Haven't you really grasped this yet? They're trigger happy and crazy. Just do as they say. Just find that damned stash!"

Something in her jaw seemed to be working. She looked away from him.

"You found it already?" he said incredulously. "You have, haven't you? But that's impossible so fast!"

She didn't confirm or deny; she gave no answer. He heard a crackle on the phone line and put it back to his ear. As he did so, he looked out the windows.

Dillinger, wielding a semiautomatic, was leading out two hostages carrying Jose Marquez. They brought him close to the gate, Dillinger keeping his weapon trained on them the entire time.

They left Jose and walked back into the house.

Dillinger followed them.

A second later the gate opened. Police rushed in and scooped up the security guard. They hurried out with him.

The gates closed and locked.

"Barrow! Barrow? Hey, you there?"

"Yes," Nick replied into the phone.

"We have the security guard. We'll get him to the hospital. What about the others? Do they need food, water?"

Kody was staring at him. He heard footsteps pounding up the stairs, as well.

Dillinger was back.

"Sit!" he told Kody. "Figure out what we need to do in order to get our hands on that stash."

To his surprise, she sat. She sat—and had the journal up in her hands before Dillinger returned to the room.

"Well?" Dillinger said to Nick.

Nick spoke into the phone. "We've given you the hostage in good faith. We really would like to see that all these good folks live, but, hey, they call bad guys bad guys because…they're bad. So back away from the gates and start making things happen. What about our boats?"

"I swear, we're getting you the best boats," Craig said.

"I want them now," Dillinger said.

"We need you to supply those boats now," Nick said, nodding to Dillinger and repeating his demand over the phone. "We need them out back, by the docks, and then we need you and your people to be far, far away."

"The boats will be there soon," Craig told Nick.

"Soon? Make that six or *seven* minutes at most!" he said.

He hoped Craig picked up on the clue. Stressing the word told him there were seven in this merry band of thieves.

"Don't push it too far!" Nick added. "Maybe we'll give you to ten or *eleven* minutes to get it together, but…well, you don't want hostages to start dying, do you?"

Easy enough. That told him there were eleven hostages, including Dakota Cameron, being held.

Dillinger looked at Nick and nodded, satisfied.

"We've got one of the boats," Craig said. "How do I get my man to bring it around and not get killed or become a hostage himself?" he asked.

"One boat?"

"So far. Getting our hands on what you want isn't easy," Craig said. "If we give you that one boat, what do we get?"

"You just got a man."

"We could find a second boat more quickly if we had a second man—or woman," Craig said.

They had to be careful; the negotiator's voice carried on the land line.

Of course, Craig Frasier knew that. He would be careful, but Nick knew that he had to be more so. Dakota could hear Craig, as well.

"Please," she said softly, "give them Stacey Carlson and Nan Masters. They're older. They'll just be like bricks around your neck when you need hostages for cover. Please, let them leave."

"Please," Dillinger said, mimicking her plea, "find what I want to know!"

"I might have," Kody said very softly.

"You might have?"

"Give the cops two more hostages. Give them Stacey and Nan," she said. "I'll show you what I think I've figured out once you've done that. Please."

Dillinger looked at Nick. "Hey, the lady said please. Let's accommodate her. Get on the phone and tell them to get the hell away from the gate. We'll give them two more solid, stand-up citizens." His eyes narrowed. "But I want my boats. Two boats. And I want them now. No ten minutes. No eleven minutes. I want them now!"

He looked at Kody. She was staring gravely at him.

"We have a present for you," he told Craig over the phone. "Two more hostages. Only we want two boats. Now. We want them right now."

"And if we don't get those boats soon…" Dillinger murmured.

He looked over at Kody.

And his eyes seemed to smile.

Chapter Three

"It's done. He's let them go. Three of the hostages. Your security man, Marquez, and the manager and his assistant."

Kody looked up from the journal she'd been reading.

Concentration had not been an easy feat; men were walking around with guns threatening to kill people. That made her task all the more impossible.

But it was Barrow who had walked in to speak with her. And the news was good. Three of her coworkers were safe.

And she was sure it was Craig Frasier out there doing the negotiating with them on the phone. Craig Frasier. From New York. In Miami.

But then, at Finnegan's, Kieran had been saying that Craig was going on the road; they'd been tracking a career criminal who'd recently gotten out of prison and was already starting up in NYC, and undercover agents in the city had warned that he was moving south.

Dillinger?

Was Craig Frasier here in Miami after Dillinger?

The masked man with the intense blue eyes was

staring at her. She schooled her expression, not wanting to give away any of her thoughts or let on that she knew the negotiator and might know about their leader.

"So what happens now?" she asked. Capone was once again standing just outside the library, near the arched doorway to the room. He was, however, out of earshot, she thought, as long as they spoke softly.

"We need getaway boats. And, of course, Anthony Green's bank haul stash. How are you doing?" Barrow asked her.

How the hell was she doing?

Maybe—*maybe*—with days or weeks to work and every bit of reference from every conceivable source, she might have an answer. So far she had found some interesting information about the old gangster, Miami in the mob heyday, and even geography. She'd gone through specs and architectural plans on the house. But she was pretty sure she'd been right from the beginning—the stash was not at the house on Crystal Island. It was in the Everglades—somewhere.

To say that to find something in the Everglades was worse than finding a needle in a haystack was just about the understatement of the year. The Everglades was actually a river—"a river of grass," as one called it. On its own, it was ever-changing. Man, dams, the surge of sugar and beef plantations from the middle of the state on down, kept the rise and flow eternally moving, right along with nature. There were hammocks or islands of high land here and there. The Everglades also offered quicksand, dangerous native snakes and now, sixty-thousand-plus pythons and boas that had been let loose in the marsh and swamps, not to mention both alligators and, down in the brackish water, crocodiles, as well.

Great place to hide something!

"Well?" Barrow asked quietly.

"I don't think the stash is here," she said honestly. "Anthony Green talks about having a shack out in the Everglades. My dad and his University of Miami buddies used to have one. They went hunting—they had their licenses and their permits to take two alligators each. But usually they just went to their shack, talked about school and sports and women—and then shot up beer cans. The shacks were outlawed twenty or thirty years ago. But that didn't mean the shacks all went down, or that some of the old-timers who run airboat rides or tours off of the Tamiami Trail don't remember where a lot of them are."

"So, the stash is in one of the old cabins," Barrow murmured. "But you don't know which—or where." He hesitated. "A place like Lost City?"

Kody stared at the man, surprised. Most of the people she knew who had grown up in the area hadn't even heard about Lost City.

Lost City was an area of about three acres, perhaps eight miles or so south of Alligator Alley, now part of I-75, a stretch of highway that crossed the state from northwestern Broward County over to the Naples/Ft. Myers area on the west coast of the state. It was suspected that Confederate soldiers had hidden out there after the Civil War, and many historians speculated that either Miccosukee or Seminole Indians had come upon them and massacred them all. Scholars believed it had been a major Seminole village at some point—and that it had been in use for hundreds of years.

But, most important, perhaps, was the fact that Al Capone—the real prohibition era gangster—had used the area to create his bootleg liquor.

She hesitated, not sure how much information to share—and how much to hold close.

Then again, she didn't have a single thing that was solid.

But…

It was evident he knew the area. Possibly, he'd grown up in South Florida, too. With the millions of people living in Miami-Dade and Broward counties alone, it was easy to believe they'd never met.

And yet, they had.

She knew his eyes.

And she had to believe that, slimy thief that he was, he was not a killer.

Yes, she had to believe it. Because she was depending on him, leaning on him, believing that he was the one who might save them—at the least, save their lives! She had to believe it because…

It wasn't right.

But, when she looked at him. When he spoke, when he made a move to protect one of them…

There was just something about him. And it made her burn inside and wish that…

Wish that he was the good guy.

"Something like that," she said, "except there's another version of the Al Capone distillery farther south.

Supposedly, Anthony Green had a spot in the Everglades where he, too, distilled liquor. Near it, he had one of the old shacks. The place is up on an old hammock and, like the Capone site, it was once a Native American village, in this case, Miccosukee."

"You know where this place is?" Barrow asked her.

"Well, theoretically," she said with a shrug. "Almost all the Everglades is part of the national parks system, or belonging to either the Miccosukee or the Seminole tribes. But from what I understand, Anthony Green had his personal distillery on a hammock in the Shark Valley Slough—which empties out when you get to the Ten Thousand Islands, which are actually in Monroe County. But I don't think that it's far from the observation tower at Shark Valley. There's a hammock—"

Kody stopped speaking when she noticed him staring down at one of the glass-framed historic notes she had set next to the Anthony Green journal she'd been cross-referencing.

"Chakaika," he said quietly.

She started, staring at him when he looked up and seemed to be smiling at her.

"A very different leader," he said. "Known as the 'Biggest Indian.' He was most likely of Spanish heritage, with mixed blood from the Creek perhaps, or another tribe that had members flee down to South Florida. Anyway, he was active from the center of the state on down—had his own mix of Spanish and Native American tongues and traded with other Native Americans, but seemed to have a hatred for the whites who wanted to ship the Indians to the west. He attacked the fort and he headed down to Pigeon Key, where he murdered Dr. Henry Perrine—who really was, by all historic record, a cool guy who just wanted to use his plants to find cures for diseases.

"Anyway, in revenge, Colonel Harney disguised himself and his men as Native Americans and brought canoes down after Chakaika, who thought they could not find him in the swamp. But they found a runaway slave of the leader's who led them right to the hammock where the man lived. They didn't let him surrender—they shot him and his braves, and then they hanged him. And the hammock became known as Hanging People Kay. I know certain park rangers believe they know exactly where it is."

Kody lowered her head, keeping silent for a minute. Her parents had been slightly crazy environmentalists. She knew all kinds of trivia about the state and its history. But while most people who had grown up down here might know the capital and the year the territory had become a state or the state bird or motto, few of them knew about Chakaika. Tourists sometimes stopped at the museum heading south on Pidgeon Key where Dr. Henry Perrine had once lived and worked, but nothing beyond that.

"Chakaika," he said again. "It's written clearly on the corner of that letter."

"Yes, well…they found oil barrels sunk in the area once," she murmured. "They were filled with two of Anthony Green's henchmen who apparently fell into ill favor with their boss. I know that the rangers out there are pretty certain they know the old Green stomping grounds—just like they know all about Chakaika. The thing is, of course, it's a river of grass. An entire ecosystem starting up at Lake Kissimmee and heading around Lake Okeechobee and down. Storms have come and gone, new drainage systems have gone in… I just don't know."

"It's enough to give him," Barrow said. "Enough to make him move."

Kody leaned forward suddenly. "You don't want to kill people. You hate the man. So why don't you shoot him in the kneecap or something?"

"And then Capone would shoot us all," Barrow said. "Do you really think that I could just gun them all down?"

"No, but you could—"

"Injure a man like that, and you might as well shoot yourself," he told her. "And, never mind. I have my reasons for doing what I'm doing. There's no other choice."

"There's always a choice," Kody said.

"No," he told her flatly, "there's not. So, if you want to keep breathing and keep all your friends alive, as well—"

Dillinger came striding in. "So, Miss Cameron. Where is my treasure?"

"Dammit! Listen to me and believe me! It's not here, not in the house, not on the island," she told him. She realized that while she was speaking fairly calmly, she was shivering, shaking from head to toe.

It was Dillinger and Barrow in the room then.

If Dillinger attacked her, what would Barrow do? Risk himself to defend her?

There certainly was no treasure at the house—other than the house itself—to give Dillinger. She'd told him the truth.

"So, where is it?" he demanded.

Thankfully he didn't seem to be surprised that it wasn't in the Crystal Manor.

"I have no guarantees for you," she said. "But I do have a working theory. This letter," she said, pausing to tap the historic, framed note that had been hand-penned by Anthony Green, "refers to the 'lovely hammock beneath the sun.' It was written to Lila Bay, Green's favorite mistress. In summary, Green tells her that when he's about on business and she's missing him, she should rest awhile in the hammock, and find there the diamond-like luster of the sun and the emerald green of the landscape."

"What's that on the corner?" Dillinger demanded suspiciously.

"It's the name of a long-ago chief or leader who was killed there. I think it was a further reference for Green when he was trying to see to it that Lila found the stash from the bank," Kody said.

Dillinger stood back, balancing the rifle he carried as he crossed his arms over his chest and stared at her.

"So, my treasure is in an alligator-laden swamp—along with rattlers, coral snakes, cottonmouths and whatever else! And we're just supposed to go out to the swamp and start digging in the saw grass and the muck?" Dillinger said.

"I'm still reading his personal references," Kody said. "But, yes. I can't put this treasure where it isn't. I'm afraid I'd falter and you'd know me for a liar in an instant."

"And you think you can find this treasure in acres of swamp land?" he asked.

Everything in Kody seemed to recoil. She shook her head. "I'm not going into the swamp. I don't care about the treasure or the stash. You do. I mean, I can keep reading and give you directions, all kinds of suggestions, but I—"

"Come on, Dillinger," Barrow said. "She'd be a pain in the ass out in the swamp!"

Dillinger turned to stare at Barrow. "She's going with us, one way or the other."

"What?" Barrow asked.

"Did you think I'm crazy? No way in hell we're leaving here without a hostage. We'll take Miss Cameron here for sure. I can't wait to see her dig in the muck and the old gator holes until she finds the diamonds and the emeralds! Come on, Barrow, you can't be that naive. They're not going to just give us speedboats. They're going to have the Coast Guard out. They're going to be following us. Now, I'm not without friends, and I'm pretty damned good at losing people who are chasing me, but...hey, you need to have a living hostage." He turned to Kody. "And, of course, Miss Cameron, if you're going to send us on a wild-goose chase, you have to understand just how it will end for you."

The house line began to ring again.

Dillinger looked at Barrow. “Get it! See if they have my boats for me now. You!” He pointed a finger at Kody. “You figure it out—or you will be the one in the snake and gator waters!”

Kody looked down quickly at the journal she was reading. She prayed he couldn’t see just how badly she was shaking.

She knew local lore. She’d walked the trails at Shark Valley. She’d driven out from the city a few times just to buy pumpkin bread at the restaurant across from the park.

But she’d never camped in the Everglades. She’d never even gotten out of her car on the trail once it had grown dark.

Tramping out in alligator- and snake-infested swamps? No way.

“Get the line,” Dillinger told Barrow again when the phone continued to ring.

Barrow answered.

“Where are the boats? We’re doing our best to make sure that this works but you need to start moving on your end. And, be warned—no cops, no Coast Guard, no nothing coming after us!” he said.

He looked over at Dillinger. “He’s getting us a pair of Donzi racers.”

“That will do,” Dillinger said. “As long as he starts getting it done. As long as he backs off some.”

“You keep your men in check—I mean stay back,” Barrow said to the person on the other end of the line.

Barrow covered the phone with his hand. “He swears they won’t fire unless they’re fired on. You’ve made that clear to the others, Dillinger, right? I don't want one of those trigger-happy psychos getting me killed."

"Hey, we fire on them, they fire back," Dillinger said with a shrug. "Like the saying goes, no one lives forever. If they shoot, they take a chance on killing a hostage!"

Barrow politely relayed Dillinger's threat. Then he walked out of the room, leaving Kody alone with Dillinger.

She kept telling herself that Craig was out there. He was playing a careful game, all that any man could do when hostages were involved.

Did Craig know she was in there? Of course, she knew him, she'd had meals with him and Kieran and the Finnegan family, and they'd talked about her home in Miami and the estate on Crystal Island with all its mob ties…

She blinked, determined that she not give anything away.

Dillinger just looked at her and tapped his fingers on the desk. "We need you, Miss Cameron. Isn't that nice? As long as you're needed, you know that you'll live. Remember that."

Then Dillinger, too, walked out of the room.

Kody looked around, wondering what was near her that might possibly be used as a weapon.

Nothing.

Nothing in the room stood up to a gun.

NICK STOOD WITH Dillinger in the ballroom—the large stretch on the left side of the house that connected two of the towers. Crown moldings and silk wallpaper made the room a work of real, old-artisan beauty, but, at the moment, it felt empty and their soft-spoken conversation seemed to echo loudly with the acoustics of the room.

"You played us all," he told Dillinger. "You made us all think that coming here was the job—that there was something here we'd be taking. In and out. Quick and easy. Round up people as a safety net and then get the hell out."

"I said the house was the key to great riches!" Dillinger said. "And this is an easy gig. We have some scared people. We have the cops keeping their distance at the gate. The guard is going to be okay. At worst, he'll have some stitches and a concussion. So, Barrow, don't be a pansy. You know what? I'm not so fond of the killing part myself. But, hell, when a job needs to be done..." He let Nick complete the thought himself.

Instead, Nick went on the offensive. "If Miss Cameron is right, we've got to go south from here and then west into the Everglades. Donzi speedboats aren't going to take us in to where we need to be. I don't think you planned this out."

"You don't think?" Dillinger said, tapping Nick on the forehead. "You don't think? Well, my friend, you're wrong. I know where Donzis won't take us—and I know where airboats will take us! I've done lots of thinking."

"This isn't an in and out!" Nick snapped.

"No. But the reward will be worth the effort."

So, Dillinger had known all along that what he'd

wanted wouldn't be found on the property. And he had other plans in the works already. Who else was in on it? Any of the men? None of them? Was Dillinger so uptight and paranoid that he hadn't trusted a single person in their group?

Nick was pretty sure he was doing a decent job of maintaining his cover while giving his real coworkers as much information as possible. Craig and their local FBI counterparts and law enforcement knew how many men were in the house—and how many hostages remained. He hadn't been able to risk a call to Craig—other than those he made as Barrow. While the agent didn't know the who, how or where, he now knew Dillinger had expected he'd have to leave the house to find his treasure. Would he assume that he'd be heading out to the Everglades, given the legends?

Dillinger had to have people lined up and waiting to help him. As he'd said, to get where they wanted to go, a Donzi would be just about worthless. They'd need an airboat.

Dillinger had no doubt been playing this game for the long run from the get-go.

It was still crazy. There was no real treasure they were taking from the house. There was just information—a major league *maybe* on where treasure might be found.

Dillinger was, in Nick's mind, extremely dangerous. He was crazy enough to have taken a house—a historic property—for what might possibly have been found in it.

And while none of them had even so much as suspected Dillinger would go off and do something like kidnap a child, he had done so—and been smug when he'd let them all know that he had the child for extra leverage.

The kid changed everything. Everything.

Nick couldn't wait for that moment when Dillinger was off guard and the others were in different places and he could take him down and then wait for the others. He couldn't risk losing Dillinger—not until he knew where the man was holding the little boy.

First thing now, though, Nick knew, was to get them all out of the house—alive.

Then he'd just have to keep Dakota Cameron—and himself—alive until Dillinger somehow slipped and told them where to find little Adrian Burke. Then he'd have to get himself and Kody away from Dillinger and whoever the hell else he had in on it and—

Baby steps, he warned himself.

"Here's the thing—we haven't done anything yet, not really," he told Dillinger. "Okay, assault—that's what they can get us on. They don't understand what we're doing, why in God's name we've taken this place, why we've taken hostages...and they really don't have anything. What you really want—what we all want—is the Anthony Green bank-job treasure. They just promised that they're getting the boats—that they'll be here right away. The young woman whose family owns this place is still reading records and I do think she's gotten something in two hours that no one else thought of in decades. Not that it doesn't mean we'll be digging in the muck forever but… I really suggest that you let more hostages go," Nick said.

"I don't know," Dillinger said. "Yeah, maybe… maybe we should get rid of that one woman—the one with the mouth on her. She might be stupid enough to attempt something."

"Good idea. Here's the thing—the hostages are weakening us. We have the hostages in the front and the front towers covered, and you've proven you have sharpshooters up there who will pick off men and happily join in a gunfight. But, with everyone moving around and everything going on, we are missing a man for sound protection in back. I'm afraid they'll eventually figure that out. Let go a few more hostages, and we'll be in a better position to control the ones we do keep."

Dillinger seemed to weigh his words.

Then they heard shots—individual rat-a-tats and then a spray of gunfire.

Dillinger swore, staring at Nick. "What the hell? What the bloody hell?"

"I guarantee you, the cops and the Feds were clean on that," Nick snapped. "One of your boys just went crazy with a pistol and an automatic."

He raced down the length of the room to the stairs to the tower. He was certain the first shots had come from that direction.

Another round of gunfire sounded. Nick ran on up the stairs.

Schultz was there, spraying rounds everywhere.

"What the hell is the matter with you?" Nick shouted.

The man was wielding a semiautomatic. He had to take great care.

Schultz gave him a wild-eyed look before he turned back to the window. Nick made a flying leap at him, hitting him in his midsection, bringing him down.

The semiautomatic went flying across the floor.

Nick rose, ready to yell at Schultz. But the man was staring up at him with swiftly glazing eyes. He was dead. A crack police marksman had evidently returned the spray of bullets with true accuracy.

"Hey, Barrow! Schultz!" Dillinger shouted from below.

Nick inhaled. He stood and went to the stairs.

"You brought in an idiot on this, Dillinger!" he called down. "They've taken down Schultz. The idiot just went crazy and the police returned his fire. A sharpshooter got him. We need to play for a little time while those boats get here. We need to let more of the hostages go—now. If they figure out just how weak we are in numbers, they might storm the house."

"They do, and everybody dies!" Dillinger swore.

"Don't think with your ass, Dillinger. We can pull this off if no one else acts like we're in the wild, wild, West! I want to live. I didn't come in on a frigging suicide mission! We came here for something. We need to keep calm and figure out the best way to get it. Let me offer up more hostages."

"The girl almost has it. We can grab up whatever journals and all she's using and take the boats. I want them now!"

"The boats are coming. Let me free a hostage!" Nick pleaded.

Dillinger was quiet for a minute. "Yeah, fine. Just one."

"Two would be better. There's a young couple down there—"

"No, only one of them. And tell the cops if another one of our number dies, they'll have all dead hostages. One way or the other!" Dillinger snapped. "Schultz is dead," he reminded Nick. "We should retaliate. Kill someone—not let them go."

Nick hurried along the hall back to the library, Dillinger close at his heels.

The phone was already ringing when they reached the room.

Dakota Cameron remained behind the library desk.

Her face was white, but rather than afraid she looked uneasy. Guilty of something.

For the moment Nick ignored her. He picked up the phone. Once again Craig was on the other end and they were going to play their parts.

"What happened?" Craig asked.

"Your people got a little carried away with fire," Nick said. "We now have a dead man. We should kill a hostage."

"No. The boats are coming. And your man started the firing. He was trying to kill people out here. Our people had to fire back."

"Do it again, the hostages die."

"We don't want to fire."

"Yeah, well, we have anxious people up here carrying semiautomatic weapons. But just to prove that we can keep our side of a bargain, we're going to give you another hostage. Then we want the boats."

"Yes, all right. That can be done."

"We'll have someone for you, so watch the gate. No tricks or someone will die."

"No tricks," Craig said.

Nick hung up. Dillinger was looking at him.

"Okay, we give them a hostage," Nick said. "Or two."

"Two? I said—"

"Two. We'll give them the sassy girl—Betsy, I think her name is—and then a guest. All right?"

"Fine. Do it," Dillinger said.

"You want me out there?" Nick asked.

"Yes, you, Mr. Diplomacy. Get out there."

Nick was surprised. "You're leaving her alone upstairs?" he asked.

"No." Dillinger looked over at Kody, smiled and headed over to her. "I'll be close. But just to be careful…" He reached into his pocket and pulled out police-issue plastic cuffs.

"Miss Cameron, one wrist will do. We just need to see that you don't leave the desk. I can attach you right here, to the very pretty little whirligig in the wood," Dillinger said.

Nick was relieved to see that Kody offered him her left wrist and just watched and waited in silence as he secured it to the desk. She didn't protest; she didn't cause trouble. She was probably just glad they were letting another hostage free.

But Nick didn't trust her. She was a fighter.

"Miss Cameron, you have all the clues, clues that are like a road map, right? You know what we need to do?" Dillinger asked her.

"I have an area. I have an idea," Kody said.

"Don't lie to me," Dillinger said.

She shook her head. "I told you—no guarantees. This treasure has been missing for decades. I believe I know where you can dig, but whether it's still there or not, I don't know. Even the earth shifts with time."

"I knew you could find it, my dear Miss Cameron!"

"Me? How did you even know I'd be here? I don't even live here anymore. I live in New York," Kody said.

"Oh, Miss Cameron. Of course, I checked out my information about the stash, the house—and you. It was possible but I doubted that the treasure would be in the house. I knew that you were here. I knew how much you loved this old house...and, yeah, I knew you'd be leaving soon. So it was time to act." He shrugged, as if he was done explaining. "Now let me get rid of your big-mouthed friend. You help me, I help you. That's the way it works."

Dillinger turned and looked at Nick.

Nick gritted down hard on his teeth.

Yeah, they'd all been taken on this one. Dillinger had known damned well that he hadn't gotten them all to take the house for the treasure.

They'd taken the house for Dakota Cameron.

Because Dillinger believed that she was the map to the treasure.

"Get going, Barrow. Do it. I'll be watching from

the top of the stairs. I mean, I really wouldn't want to leave Miss Cameron completely alone," Dillinger said.

Nick headed on out and down the sweeping marble stairs to the first floor.

He was loath to leave the upstairs, especially now that Schultz had been killed. He was afraid Dillinger would lose all logic in a frenzied moment of anger and start shooting.

But he had no choice. And Dillinger needed Kody Cameron. He wouldn't hurt her.

Dillinger was at the top of the stairs.

Watching Kody.

Watching Nick.

And there was nothing to do but play out the man's game…

And make it to the finish line.

Chapter Four

Capone and Nelson were with the hostages when Nick arrived in the living room. The group of them was still huddled together.

The group, at least, was a little smaller now.

"You," he said quietly, pointing at the tiny woman who had given them the hardest time. "What's your name?"

"What's it to you?" she demanded.

He fired his gun—aiming at a mirror on the wall.

It exploded. He waited in silence.

"Betsy Rodriguez!" the young woman answered him.

"Thank you," he told her. "Come on."

"What?" she asked.

"Come on. You're going out."

"Me. Just me?"

"No," he said and pointed to another young woman. She appeared to be in her mid- to late-twenties; she was clinging to the arm of the man beside her. They were a couple. It was going to be hard to split them up.

But it was what Dillinger wanted.

"You," he said to the young woman.

"Us?" she asked. As he'd expected, she didn't want to be separated from the man she was with.

"No. Just you," he said softly.

The young woman began to sob. "No," she said stubbornly. "No, no, no!"

"Please, miss," Nick said. "Honestly, none of us wants any of you dead. Help me try to see that no one does wind up dead."

"Go, Melissa, please go," the dark-haired man who was with her said. "Go!" he told her. "Please. I need to know that you're all right."

"Victor, I can't leave you," the woman—whom he now knew to be named Melissa—said.

Melissa hugged the man she had called Victor. He pulled away from her, saying, "You can and you must."

"How touching! How sweet!" Capone said.

"Nauseating!" Nelson agreed. He walked over as if about to strike one of them with the butt of his gun.

Nick moved more quickly, walking through the huddled crowd to reach Melissa and pull her to her feet. He looked down at Victor as he did so. There was something cold and hateful in the man's eyes. Cold, hateful—and oddly calm.

The guy was a cop! Nick thought. Some kind of a cop or law enforcement. He just knew it. He also knew the man wasn't going to cause trouble when he couldn't win.

Nick thought about the situation quickly. It would be good to have another cop around—except this guy didn't know that he was FBI and he could easily kill

Nick thinking he was with the bad guys—which he was, by all appearances.

He reached down and grasped the man's arm.

"Victor, you're coming, too."

The man stood and looked at him. "No, don't take me. Take the young woman who is one of the guides here. She's very scared. I'm scared—just not as scared," Victor said.

Nick liked him.

He wished he could keep him around, that they were in a situation where they could trust one another.

They weren't.

"No, I think we're going to let you lovebirds go together. I don't want my friends here becoming nauseated."

"Hey!" Nelson said. "He told you to go. You don't want us shooting up your lovey-dovey young wife, do you?"

Staring at Nick with a gaze that could cut steel, Victor took his wife's arm and started out of the room, followed by Betsy Rodriguez and then Nick.

He had to be careful now. Dillinger was watching from upstairs and Nelson was following him out to the porch.

Nick walked out toward the gate, making his way slightly past Betsy Rodriguez. He came as close to Victor as he dared and spoke swiftly.

"Cop? Please, for the love of God, tell me the truth," Nick said urgently.

Victor stared at him and then nodded.

"Tell Agent Frasier that the main man plans to get

out to the Everglades, down south of the Trail, near Shark Valley. Keep his distance. Watch for men abetting along the way."

It was all he dared say. He shoved the man forward, shouting to the assembled police, agents and whoever else at the gate, "Get the hell back! Take these three—and remember, sharpshooters have a bead on you and inside there are a few guns aimed at the skulls of a few hostages."

Craig Frasier stepped forward, his hands raised, showing that he was unarmed.

"No trouble! And boats will show up at the docks almost as we speak. But what's the guarantee for the rest of the hostages?"

"You'll find them once we're gone. Most of them," he added quietly. "But we need assurances that we won't be followed. Get too close and— Well, just keep your distance."

He stepped back behind the gate and locked it again.

Betsy Rodriguez and Melissa went running toward officers who were waiting to greet them with blankets.

Only Victor held back a moment, nodding imperceptibly to Nick.

"Wait!" Craig called. "I need more…more on the hostages to give you the two boats."

"As soon as I can see them from the back, I'll bring out a few more," he promised.

"I'll be here. Waiting."

Nick nodded gravely. He turned and headed back toward the house.

As he'd suspected, Capone had waited and watched from the porch.

Nelson was with the rest of the hostages. Dillinger was still upstairs and Floyd and Kelly would be manning the towers.

He doubted that anyone other than himself and Dillinger knew Schultz was dead. Dillinger wouldn't have shared that news, fearing the others might have wanted revenge.

Dillinger only wanted one thing: the treasure.

Capone walked with him through the grand foyer and into the music room. "Good call, by the way, on getting rid of that cop," Capone said.

Nick looked at him; Capone was no idiot. "You saw that, too?"

"Yep. That kind of guy is dangerous. We don't want any heroes around here, you know."

"No heroes," Nick agreed. He shook his head. "I've got to admit—it's got me a little worried. Getting out of here, I mean." He hesitated. A man really wouldn't want to be bad-talking an accomplice in an evil deed. "I kind of thought that Dillinger was sure what he wanted was here. I guess he had the idea we might be heading someplace else to find it all along—and that's why he took the kid. More leverage."

"Yeah, I'm figuring that's the leverage he's using to get us all out of here. Do the cops even know he's the one who took the boy?" Capone asked. "You know, I've done some bad things, but I've never hurt a kid. That's why he didn't tell us. Hell, even in prison, the men who hurt, kill or molest kids are the ones in trouble. I'd never hurt a kid!"

"Nor would I—and probably not our other guys, either, but who knows. And I don't know if the cops know that Dillinger took the boy yet, but I'm figuring they do. And if they find the kid…"

"If they find the kid, we may all be screwed," Capone said.

"Do you know where he stashed him?"

Capone shrugged. "He didn't tell me. Dillinger isn't the trusting kind. Let's just hope he knows what the hell he's doing."

Nick nodded.

He really hoped to hell he knew what he was doing himself.

KODY HAD A letter opener.

Not just any letter opener, she told herself. This was a letter opener that was now considered a historic or collectible piece. It was fashioned to look like a shiv—the same kind of weapon often carried by Anthony Green and his thugs. They'd been sold at almost every tourist shop in Miami right after Green had been gunned down on the beach.

Now, they were rare. And collectible.

And she had slid the one the property had proudly displayed on the library desk into the pocket of her jeans.

Yep, she thought, a letter opener. Against automatic weapons. Still, it was something.

Maybe it would help once they got to the Everglades.

She didn't imagine it would do much against a full-size alligator if one came upon her while she was trying to find the place in the glades where Anthony Green might have hidden his stash—or even one of the thousands of pythons. But at least it was something.

She looked up as Dillinger came striding back into the room.

"How are you doing?" he asked her.

She stared back at him. "Um, just great?" she suggested.

He laughed softly. "You are something, Miss Cameron. You see, I do know what I'm doing. I know that you know what you're doing. See, if you were to go online and Google yourself, you'd find some of your acting pages or your SAG page or whatever it is, and you'd find some promo pictures and play reviews and things like that. But when you keep going, you find out that you were quite the little writer when you were in college and that you did a feature for the school paper on the mob in Miami. You'd already done a lot of studying up on Anthony Green—and why not? Your dad inherited this place! Now, of course, I know you're not rich, that he runs it all in a trust. But I knew that if anyone knew how to get rich, it would be you. As in—if anyone could find the stash, it would be you."

Kody tried not to blink too much as she looked back at him. The man wasn't just scary. He was creepy. He was some kind of an intellectual stalker—and knew things about her that she'd half forgotten herself. It was terrifying to realize he'd really gone on a cyber-hunt for her—and that he'd found far more than most people would ever want to find.

Her skin seemed to crawl.

"I keep telling you this—there's no guarantee. Most people who have studied Anthony Green and Crystal Island and even the mob in general have believed that Green stashed his treasure out in the Everglades. I think I've found verification of that—and that's all," she said.

"But you know just about where. Everyone has looked around Shark Valley—but you know more precisely where. Because you also studied the Seminole Wars, and you loved the Tamiami Trail growing up—and made your parents drive you back and forth from the east to the west of the Florida peninsula all the time."

"I didn't make them," Kody protested, noting how ridiculous her words were under the circumstances. "And you really are counting on what may not exist at all."

"The stash exists!"

"Unless it was found years ago. Unless it's sunk so deep no one will ever find it. Oh, my God, come on! Criminals have written volumes on people killed and tossed into the Everglades, criminals through time who never did a day of time because the Everglades can hide just about anything—and anyone! I can try. I can try with everything I've learned now that I've been put to the fire, and everything that I know from what I've heard and what I've read through the years. But—"

She broke off. He was, she was certain, smiling—even if she couldn't exactly see his face.

"That's right," he said softly. "Bodies have disappeared out there. You might want to remember that."

"Maybe you should remember not to threaten people and scare them and make them totally unnerved when you want them to do calculated thinking!" she countered quickly.

He held still, quiet for a minute. "It will be fun when we reach the peak, Miss Cameron. It will be fun," he promised.

Ice seemed to stir and settle in her veins.

It would be fun...

He meant to kill her.

And still, she'd play it out. Right now, of course, because many lives were resting on her managing to keep this man believing...

And then, of course, because her life depended on it.

Barrow came striding into the room, his blue eyes blazing from his mask. As they lit on her, she felt the intensity of their stare and once again she had a strange feeling that she'd been touched by those eyes before.

"We're closing in on time to go. What are you going to need here, Miss Cameron?" he asked. Then he turned to Dillinger. "I'd wrap up whatever books and journals she wants to take. We'll be getting wet, getting out of here in speedboats."

"Well, what do you need, Miss Cameron?" Dillinger asked.

Barrow had walked over to the windows that looked out over the water.

“They’re coming now,” he said.

Dillinger walked over to join him. “They’ve stopped about a mile out.”

“I’ll give them a few more people and they’ll bring the boats in to the docks. Their people will clear the area and we’ll leave the last of the hostages on the dock for them,” Barrow said.

“Not good enough,” Dillinger said. “We need at least a couple of them with us.”

“All right, how’s this? We let three go. We take two with us—and leave them off once we’re a safe distance away.”

“I say when it’s a safe distance. And if they follow us, the hostages are dead,” Dillinger said flatly.

“I’m telling you, hostages will be like bricks around our necks once we start moving,” Barrow said.

“Let the guests go. There are a couple of people who work here left—keep them,” Dillinger said.

Kody jumped up. “If you’re taking them, let me talk to my friends. The guides who work here. Let me talk to them. It will make it easier for you.”

Dillinger pulled out a knife. For a moment she thought that Barrow was going to fly across the room and stop him from stabbing her.

But he didn’t intend to stab her.

He cut through the plastic cuffs that held her to the desk.

“Go down. I’ll warn our guys in the turrets about what’s going on,” he said.

Barrow caught Kody by the arm. She wanted to wrench free but she didn’t. She felt the strength of his hold—and the pressure of her shiv letter opener in her pocket.

She glanced at him as they headed down the stairs.

"This isn't the time," he said.

"The time for what?"

"Any kind of trick."

"I wasn't planning one, but if I had, wouldn't this be the right time—I mean, before we're in a bog or marsh and saw grass and Dillinger shoots me down?"

Those blue eyes of his lit on her with the strangest assessment.

"Now is not the time," he repeated.

She looked away quickly. The man put out such mixed signals. He didn't like blood and guts, yet he didn't want any escape attempts.

He headed with her into the music room where they joined Capone and Nelson.

"You, you, and you!" he said, pointing out the two male and the one female guests.

They stood, looking at one another anxiously. Kody was amazed at how clearly she remembered their names now. The men were Gary Goodwin and Kevin Dean. The woman was Carey Herring.

"No, no, no! They're getting out—and we're not!"

Kody turned quickly to see that Brandi Johnson, her face damp with tears, was looking at the trio who was then standing.

She left Barrow's side, hurrying over to the young woman. "It's okay. It's okay, Brandi," she said. She squeezed the girl's hand and then pulled her close, talking to her and to the young man with the thick glasses at her side. "Brandi, Vince, we're all going to be together. We're going to be fine. Don't you worry. They need us."

"I'm good, Kody. I'm good," Vince told her. She smiled at him grimly. She really loved Vince; he was as smart as a whip and loved everything about his job at the estate. He had contacts that he seldom wore and he was a runner—a marathon runner. He'd told her once that he liked to look like a nerd—which, of course, he was, in a way—because nerds were in.

He would be good to have at her side. Except…

She was very afraid that Brandi was right; they were the ones who would end up dead.

But not now. Right now, she was still needed. All she had to do was to make sure that Dillinger believed they could all be important in finding his precious Anthony Green treasure.

"Come on, you three, it's your lucky day," Barrow said quietly to the guests. "Let's go."

Kody stayed behind with the two guides, taking their arms in hers. "Just hang tight with me," she whispered to a trembling Brandi.

"Stop it. Move away from each other," Nelson told them.

"She's scared!" Kody informed him. "We're not doing anything. She's just scared."

Barrow—who almost had the three being released out the door—paused and looked back. "They're okay, Nelson. Trust me." He turned to Kody. "No tricks at this moment in time, right?"

She met those eyes and, for whatever reason, she had a feeling he was giving her advice she needed to heed. “No tricks.”

ALL THE WAY to the gate, the young woman who was being set free looked back at Nick, tripped and had to grasp someone to keep standing.

“We’re almost at the gate,” Nick told her. “Look, it’s all right. You’re going!”

“Someone is going to shoot me in the back!” she whispered tearfully.

“No, you’re safe. You’re out of here.”

When he got the gate open, Craig Frasier raised his arms to show that he was unarmed then stepped forward to accept the hostages.

As he did so, they heard a short blast of gunfire.

“What the hell!” Nick muttered, spinning around furiously. The angle meant the shot had come from one of the towers—and it hadn’t been aimed at one of the hostages, him or Craig.

The shot had been aimed at the sky.

Dillinger. He’d headed up to one of the towers himself.

He leaned out over the coral rock balustrade to shout out to the FBI.

“We’ve got three young people left. They will die if you don’t back off completely. You follow us, they die. It’s that simple. Do you understand?”

Craig pushed the three hostages through the gate, then stepped back from the fence, lifting his hands.

"We aren't following. How do we get the last three?" he shouted.

"We'll call you. Give Barrow there a number. If we get out safe and sound, they'll be safe. Even deal. Got it?"

Craig reached into his pocket and handed Nick his card. Nick shoved the card into the pocket of his shirt. Barely perceptible, Craig nodded. Then he shouted again, calling out to Dillinger, "You have someone else. The boy that was kidnapped this morning. When are you going to give us the boy?"

For a moment Dillinger was silent. Then he spoke.

"When I'm ready. When you keep your word. When you get these hostages back, you'll know how to find the boy."

"Give us the boy now—in good faith. He's just a kid," Craig said, looking at Nick for some sign. But Nick shook his head. So far, he hadn't gotten Dillinger to say anything.

"Kids are resilient!" Dillinger called. "You keep your word, you get the kid."

Craig looked at Nick again. Nick did his best to silently convey the fact that he knew it was imperative they keep everyone alive—and that he figured out where Dillinger had stashed Adrian Burke before it was too late.

The cop—Victor Arden—had apparently repeated word for word what Nick had said earlier. Craig knew what Nick knew so far; they wouldn't have to follow the Donzis at a discreet distance. Dillinger would take his band the sixty-plus miles from their location there on the island down and around the peninsula, curving around Homestead and Florida City, to Everglades National Park.

Every available law-enforcement officer from every agency—Coast Guard, U.S. Marshals, State Police, Rangers, FBI, Miccosukee Police and so forth—would be on the lookout. At a distance.

While that was promising, the sheer size of the Everglades kept Nick from having a good feeling. Too many people got lost in the great "river of grass" and were never seen again.

He needed to actually speak with Craig—without being watched or heard.

"The boats are docking now in back," Craig told him. "How will my men get back?" He looked up at the tower and raised his voice. "If they're assaulted in any way—"

A shot was fired—into the sky once again.

And Dillinger spoke, shouting out his words. "They just walk off onto the dock. You stay where you are. My friend, Mr. Barrow there, is going to walk around and bring them to you. You know that I have sharpshooters up here in the towers. No tricks. Hey, if I'm going to die here today, everybody can die here today!"

"We don't want anyone to die," Craig said.

"So, my boats best not run out of gas," Dillinger said. "Fix it now…or a hostage dies, I guarantee you."

"You're not going to run out of gas. You have good boats, in sound working order," Craig promised him. "My men will leave the boats' keys in the ignitions, and give Barrow here backups. As soon as my men are safely off the property, we'll all back away."

"Go get 'em, Barrow!" Dillinger shouted.

Nick backed away from the fence and then turned to follow the tile path around the house and out to the back. He traversed the gardens to the docks.

There were two Donzis there, both a good size, both compact and tight. They were exactly what Dillinger had wanted.

Two men, Metro-Dade police, Nick thought, leaped up onto the dock as they saw Nick. They eyed him carefully as he came to meet them. He figured they knew his undercover part in this, but they would still carry out the charade for his safety.

He reached for the keys then he pretended to jerk the two men around and push them forward. He lowered his head and spoke softly. "Tell Frasier and the powers that be to concentrate south of Shark Valley. Around Anthony Green's old distillery grounds."

"Gotcha," one of the men murmured, turning back to look at Nick and raise his hands higher, as if trying to make sure Nick wouldn't shoot him.

"They're after Green's treasure?" the second man asked, incredulous. "Asses!" he murmured. "Everyone is still…okay?"

"Yeah. I'm trying to keep it that way," Nick said. He fell silent. They had come closer to the house on the path. In a few steps they'd be turning the corner to the front. He couldn't risk Dillinger so much as looking at his lip movement suspiciously.

He got the two men to the gate, opened it and shoved them out.

He carefully locked the gate again, looking at Craig.

There was no shout and there were no instructions from the tower. Dillinger, he knew, had already moved on. He'd have gotten what books and materials Dakota Cameron was using and he'd have headed on down and out.

Nick walked backward for a few minutes and then headed back into the house.

As he'd expected, it was empty.

He went through the music room, checked the courtyard and made his way through the vast back porch to look out to the docks.

The cons were already on their way to the boats with the hostages. Dillinger himself was escorting Kody Cameron.

Nick reached the docks just as Dillinger was handing out boat assignments.

Nelson, Capone, Kelly and the young woman, Brandi Johnson, were to take one boat.

Dillinger would take the second with Floyd, Vince and Kody Cameron.

And Barrow, of course.

"Barrow, move it!"

"No!" Brandi cried, trying to break free from Capone to reach Kody and Vince. "No, please, no. Please don't make me be alone, please..."

"You don't need to be alone. I can shoot you right here," Dillinger said.

"Then you can shoot me, too!" Kody snapped. "You

let her come with us or you let me go with her, one or the other!"

"I should shoot you!" Dillinger flared, gripping Kody by the front of her tailored shirt.

"Hey!" Barrow stepped in, extracting Kody from Dillinger's grip—a little less than gently—and staring down Dillinger. "Eyes on the prize, remember? Can we get out of here, dammit! Let's go while the going is good. Vince, just go with the nice Mr. Nelson, nice Mr. Capone, and nice Mr. Kelly, please. Brandi—Miss Johnson, step aboard that boat, please!"

Everyone seemed to freeze in response to his words to Dillinger for a minute.

Then Dillinger ripped off his cheap costume shop mask and glared around at everyone.

Nick had his hand on Kody's arm. He could feel the trembling that began.

Now they all knew what Dillinger looked like. They could identify him. Until now, the hostages weren't at much of a risk.

Now they were.

"What are you doing?" Capone began.

"What's the difference?" Dillinger spat. "Who cares? We'll be long gone, and we'll leave these guys in the Everglades. By the time they're found—if they're found—we'll be gone."

The others hesitated and then took off their masks.

And Barrow had no choice. He took off his mask and stared at Kody—praying.

The instant he pulled it off, he detected the flare in her eyes.

She recognized him, of course. Knew that she knew him…immediately. He'd always had the feeling she'd suspected he was familiar, but now that she could see his face, she was certain.

But from the look of confusion that overtook her face, he knew she couldn't place him exactly. And if she did figure it out, he'd have to pray she was bright enough to not say anything. She had to be. Both their lives depended on it.

"Let's get going!"

Nick moved them along, hopping into the front Donzi himself without giving Dillinger a chance to protest.

Dillinger followed, allowing his changes.

Nick turned the key in the ignition, shouting back to Capone after his boat roared to life, "You good back there?"

"She's purring like a kitten!" Capone called to him.

Nick led the way. He looked anxiously to the horizon and the shoreline. He skirted the other islands, shot under the causeway, joining the numerous other boats.

There was no way to tell which might be pleasure boats and which might be police. He had to trust in Craig to see that law enforcement got in front of them, that officers would be in the Everglades to greet them.

He drove hard for forty-five minutes. The day was cool and clear; under different circumstances, it would have been a beautiful day for boating.

Dillinger suddenly stood by him at the helm. "Cut the motor!" he commanded.

"I thought you wanted—"

"Cut the motor!"

Nick did so. "What are you doing?"

"See that fine-looking vessel up there? Not quite a yacht, but I'd say she's a good thirty feet of sleek speed."

"Yeah, so?"

"We're taking her."

"Ah, come on, Dillinger! She's not the prize," Nick protested.

The second Donzi came up next to them. "That one?" Kelly shouted to Dillinger.

"Looks good to me," Dillinger shouted back.

Nick realized they'd come up with this game plan while he'd been working with the hostages.

"No," Nick said. "No, no, this isn't good."

"What are you, an ass?" Dillinger asked him. "You don't think the cops won't be looking for these Donzis soon enough? Even if they know we have hostages—even they know I took the kid. We're taking that boat!"

Kelly was already moving his boat around the larger vessel. He started shouting. A grizzly-looking fellow with bright red skin and a captain's hat appeared at the rail. "What the hell are you carrying on about, boy?" he demanded.

Kelly lifted his semiautomatic and pointed it at the old man. "Move over, sir! We're coming aboard!"

"Son of a bitch!" Nick roared. He kicked his vessel back into gear, flooring it on a course toward the second Donzi.

Kelly turned to him, gun in hand.

"What the hell is the matter with you?" Nick demanded of Kelly.

"What the hell is the matter with *you*?" Dillinger asked him.

"We're not killing the old bastard," Nick said, snapping his head around to stare at Dillinger. "We're not doing it. I am not risking a death penalty for you stupid asses!"

Huddled together in the seat that skirted the wheel, Kody and Brandi Johnson were staring at him.

For the moment, he ignored them.

They were safe for now.

The old man wasn't.

Not giving a damn about damage or bumpers, Nick shoved the Donzi close to the larger vessel; she was called *Lady Tranquility.*

Nick found a hold on the hull and lifted himself up and over onto the deck. The old man just stared at him, shaking his head. "You think I'm grateful? You think I'm grateful you didn't kill me? You're still a thug. And you should still be strung up by the heels."

"You got a dinghy of any kind?" Nick asked, ignoring him.

"Yeah, I got a blow-up emergency boat."

"This is an emergency. Blow it up and get the hell out of here!" Nick said.

By then, he heard Dillinger yelling at him again. Floyd was coming up on board, using a cleat the same way Nick had, and Dillinger was pushing Kody upward.

He helped Floyd on, and Kody, and then Brandi.

"Get him in his inflatable dinghy and get him out of here!" Nick urged Floyd.

Floyd stared at him. Then he shrugged and grabbed the old man. "Let's do it, you old salt. Let's do it."

"Make sure he stays the hell away from the radio!" Dillinger ordered, crawling up onto the deck at last. "Come on, get on up here!" Dillinger called to the men in the second Donzi.

Nick left them at the bow, heading toward the aft. He got a quick look down the few stairs that led to the cabin. Seemed there was a galley, dining area, couches—and a sleeping cabin beyond.

The storage was aft; the old man had gotten his inflatable out.

Floyd was keeping an eye on him. "Hurry it up, geezer!" Floyd commanded.

Nick took a quick look down into the cabin and toyed with the idea of using the radio quickly. He made it down the steps, but heard movement above.

"Who the hell does he think he is?" Nick heard. It was Kelly—and he was furious that Nick had stopped him. "Like he thinks he's the boss? Well, the pansy sure as hell isn't my boss!"

Nick looked up the stairs and saw Kelly's gun aimed at the old man again.

Nick couldn't shoot but he couldn't let the man die. His hand reached out for the nearest weapon—a frying pan that hung on a hook above the galley sink. He grabbed it in an instant and aimed it at Kelly's head.

His aim was good—and the old frying pan was

solid. Kelly stumbled right to the portside and over the deck and into the water.

Floyd stared at him.

"We're not killing anyone!" Nick snapped.

Floyd shrugged and turned to the old man. "Better get in that boat, then, mister. If he's alive, Kelly will be coming back meaner than hell."

Nick looked at Floyd.

Floyd wasn't a killer, he realized.

Good to know.

Of course, Floyd wasn't a model of citizenry, either.

It was still good to know that in this number, there was at least one more man who didn't want the bay to run red with blood.

"Hey, Barrow!"

It was Dillinger shouting for him. He hurried around to the front.

"Get her moving!" Dillinger said.

"Aye, aye, sir," Nick said. He hurried back to the helm, set the motor and turned the great wheel.

A minute later Dillinger came and stood by him. "Hey, where the hell is Kelly?"

Nick tensed. "I think he went for a swim." Dillinger was silent.

"Hmm. At this point, good riddance." Dillinger shrugged and then turned toward the cabin. "Well, I'll bet the old guy didn't know much about fine wine, but there's bound to be some beer aboard. You know the course, right? Hold to it. We'll be around the bend to some mangrove swamps I know and love soon enough."

Dillinger left him, heading down to the cabin.

Nick spared a moment to take stock. This mission was definitely not going the way they'd planned when he'd signed on to go undercover. But he was playing the hand he'd been dealt. He had no other choice.

At least they were down to three hostages. Dakota Cameron, Brandi Johnson and Vince Jenkins.

And down to four cons. Nelson, Capone, Floyd and Dillinger.

And, of course, there was still a kidnapped boy out there…

And they were heading for the Everglades. Where, soon enough, the winter sun would set.

Chapter Five

"God, it's dark!" Brandi whispered to Kody.

"Yes, it's dark," Kody whispered back. She wasn't sure why they were whispering. She, Vince and Brandi were the only ones down in the cabin. They were hardly sharing any type of useful secrets.

Above them, on deck, were their captors. Men she could see clearly now.

Dillinger, the oldest and the craziest in the group, had a lean face with hollow cheeks, and eyes that darted in a way that made her think of a gecko. Floyd was almost as much of a "pretty boy" as his borrowed gangster name implied. Nelson, also whipcord-lean, tense, reminded her of a very nervous poodle. Capone was muscular and somewhat stout, with brown eyes and chubby cheeks.

And Barrow.

Yes, she knew him. She knew his face. She recognized him.

From where? She still couldn't pinpoint just when she'd seen him before. So how could she possibly be so certain they had met? But she was.

Why did she feel a strange sense of attraction to him, as if he were some kind of an old friend, or an acquaintance, or even someone she had seen and thought…

I need to know him.

"Where are we? Do you think we're still in Florida?" Brandi asked. "I mean…we're on the water, I know that, but we're not really moving anymore. I don't think. Or we're going really slow."

"We're right off the tip of the peninsula," Vince said. "Kind of out in the swamps that would make us really hard to find. But, in truth, a pretty cool place, really. You know crocodiles usually hang out in salt water, and alligators like fresh water, but here, we have both—yeah, both. Alligators and crocodiles. 'Cause of the way the Everglades is like a river of grass, you got the brackish thing going…"

Brandi was staring at him in horror.

Kody set a hand on his arm. "Come on, all three of us grew up here. I know I've been to Shark Valley a couple of dozen times. The wildlife is just there—snakes and alligators in the canals and on the trails—and people don't bother them and they don't bother people. We're going to be fine," she told Brandi.

"They're going to leave us out here, aren't they?" she asked, tilting her head to indicate the men on the deck.

"Don't be silly," Kody said.

"Yeah, don't be silly," Vince said. "They're not going to leave us—not alive anyway."

Brandi let out a whimper; Kody pulled her in close and glared at Vince.

"Sorry!" he whispered. "But, really, what do you think is going on?"

"I don't know," Kody admitted.

Vince looked over at her, obviously sorry he'd been so pessimistic when Brandi was barely hanging in.

"I've come down this way a lot," he said. "Hop on the turnpike and take it all the way down to Florida City, hop off, take a right and you get to the Ernest F. Coe Visitor Center, or head a little farther west and go to the Royal Palm Visitor Center and you can take the Anhinga Trail walk and see some of the most amazing and spectacular birds ever!"

Brandi turned and looked at him sourly. "Birds. Yep, great. Birds."

Vince looked at Kody a little desperately.

"Let me see what's going on," she whispered.

She left her position at the main cabin's table and inched her way to the stairs.

As she did so, she heard a long, terrified scream. She ran up the few stairs to reach the deck and paused right when she could see the men. Vince and Brandi came up behind her, shoving her forward so that she nearly lost her balance as the three of them landed on the highest step.

"What the hell?" Dillinger demanded angrily.

Yeah, what the hell? Kody wondered.

The boat's lights cast off a little glow but beyond that the world seemed ridiculously dark out on the water. Except, of course, Kody realized, the moon was out—and it was high up in the sky, bathing in soft light the growth of mangroves, lilies, pines and whatever else had taken root around them.

Kody wasn't a boater, or a nature freak. But she did know enough to be pretty sure they were hugging a mangrove shoreline and that the boat they were on had basically run aground—if that was what you called it when you tangled up in the mangrove roots.

And now it appeared that Nelson was heading back to the boat across the water, walking—or rather running—on water. He wasn't, of course. He was moving across submerged roots and branches and the build-up of sediment that occurred when the trees, sometimes in conjunction with oyster beds, formed coastlines and islands.

"What the hell are you doing, running like a slimy coward?" Dillinger thundered. "Where the hell is Capone?"

"Back there… We were shining the lights and trying to see around us but it's pitch-dark out here. We were a few feet apart. We kept flashing the lights, trying to attract your friend who is supposed to come help us, just like you told us… There was a huge splash, a huge splash, can't tell you how it sounded," Nelson said. He held a gun. He was shaking so badly, Kody was afraid he'd shoot somebody by accident. He worked his jaw and kept speaking. "I saw…I saw eyes. Like the devil's eyes. I heard Capone scream…it was…it was…not much of a scream…a choking scream… It's out there. A monster. And it got him. It got Capone."

"You mean you two were attacked by the wildlife and you just left Capone out there to fight it alone? You have a gun! No, wait! You don't just have a gun—you have an automatic!"

"I couldn't see a damned thing. I couldn't shoot—I couldn't shoot. I could have hit Capone."

"You left Capone!" Dillinger said.

Nelson stared back at him. "Yeah, I left Capone. He was—he was being eaten. He was dead. Dead already. There wasn't anything I could have done."

Kody heard a shot ring out. She saw Nelson continue to stare at Dillinger as if he was in shock. Then, he keeled over backward, right over the hull of the boat, gripping his chest as blood spewed from it.

He crashed into the water.

And Brandi began to scream.

Dillinger spun around. "Shut her up!" he ordered. He was still holding his smoking gun.

Kody was ice cold herself, shaking and terrified. She turned to Brandi and pulled her against her, begging, "Stop, Brandi. Stop, please!"

Vince caught hold of Brandi, pulling her back down the stairs to the cabin, out of harm's way.

There was silence on deck then.

Barrow, Floyd and Dillinger—and Kody—stood there in silence, staring at one another.

"He was one of us!" Floyd said.

"He wasn't one of us!" Dillinger argued. "He let a prehistoric monster eat Capone, eat my friend." He swore savagely and then continued. "Capone was my friend. My real friend. And that idiot led him right into the jaws of a croc or gator or whatever the hell it was!"

"I don't think it was his fault," Floyd said. "I mean—"

Dillinger raised his gun again. Barrow stepped between the two men, reaching out to set his hand on the barrel of Dillinger's gun and press it downward.

"Stop," Barrow said. "Stop this here and now. What's happened has happened. No more killing!"

Dillinger stared at Barrow. Maybe even he saw Barrow as the one voice of sanity in the chaos of their situation.

But, Kody realized, she was still shaking herself. Cold—and shaking so badly she could hardly remain on her feet.

She shouldn't be so horrified; the two dead men were criminals. Criminals who had been threatening her life.

But it was still horrible. Horrible to think that a man had been eaten alive. Horrible to have watched a man's face as a bullet hit his chest, as he splashed over into the water…

"I never heard such a thing," Floyd murmured as if speaking to himself. "An alligator taking a full-grown man like that."

"Maybe that idiot Nelson panicked too soon and Capone is still out there?" Dillinger asked.

Kody jerked around, startled when she heard Vince speaking from behind her.

"In the Everglades, alligator attacks on humans are very rare. I think the worst year was supposed to be back in 2001. Sixteen attacks, three fatal. You know all those things you see on TV about killer crocodilians are usually filmed in Africa along the Nile somewhere. Crocs are known to be more aggressive, and of course, we do have them here, but... Capone is a big man...not at all usual." He spoke in a monotone; probably as stunned as she was by the events in the last few minutes.

"Someone has to look," Dillinger said. "The airboat is still due. Someone has to look, has to find Capone. Has to make sure..."

No one volunteered.

"Go," Dillinger told Barrow.

"What about the hostages? Three of them and three of us," Barrow noted.

Kody had to wonder if he was worried about Dillinger managing the hostages—or if he was afraid for the hostages.

"I've got the hostages," Dillinger said. "Floyd is here with me. We're good. Go on, Barrow. You're the one with the steel balls—get out there. Find Capone. See if—"

"Alligators drown their victims. They twist them around and around until they drown them," Vince offered.

Kody gave him a good shove in the ribs with her elbow.

He fell silent.

Luckily, Dillinger hadn't seemed to have heard him.

Barrow had.

He suddenly turned and pointed at Vince. "Right, you know a fair amount, so it seems. You come with me."

Kody could feel Vince's tension. Huddled behind him, Brandi whimpered.

Kody had to wonder if Barrow hadn't told Vince

to come with him because he was afraid for Vince—afraid that Vince would say something that would send Dillinger into a fit of rage again.

"Um…all right," Vince said.

He looked at Kody, his eyes wide with fear. But then, as he stared at her, something in him seemed to change. As if, maybe, he'd realized himself that Barrow was actually trying to keep them all alive. He smiled. He crawled on past her up the rest of the cabin steps and out onto the deck.

Barrow was already crawling over the hull.

"There's a good tangle of roots right here," Barrow said. "Watch your step, and cling to the trees this way. Dillinger!"

"Yeah?" Dillinger asked.

"The boat's spotlight—throw it in that direction," Barrow said.

"Yeah, yeah, should have done that before."

Kody heard some splashes. For a few minutes she could see Barrow leading, Vince following, and the two men walking off into the mangrove swamp. Then they disappeared into the darkness of the night.

Everything seemed still, except for the constant low hum of insects…

And the occasional sound of something, somewhere, splashing the water.

Victim or prey.

"THEY REALLY DON'T," Vince said, his voice still a monotone as he followed Nick across the mangroves, slipping and sliding into several feet of water here and there. "Alligators, I mean. They don't usually attack people. We're not a good food supply. And since the python invasion down here, gators don't get big enough anymore."

"Tell that to the alligators," Nick murmured. He didn't know what the hell had happened himself. It was unlikely that a man Capone's size had been taken down by an alligator, but it wasn't impossible.

And he didn't know who the hell Dillinger was supposed to be meeting, but it was someone coming with an airboat.

Dillinger had taken over at the helm once they'd headed around the tip of the peninsula; Nick had known that he'd force them to come aground. But Dillinger had a one-track thing going with his mind. There'd been no stopping him.

Now, of course, he'd taken Vince with him to keep him alive. Dillinger was trigger happy at the moment.

Nick had been stunned himself when Dillinger had gunned down Nelson without blinking. They were all at risk. What he really needed to do was to take Dillinger down. Take him out of the equation altogether—no matter what it took.

But what about the boy? Adrian Burke. Where was the child? Only Dillinger knew.

Then again, what about the hostages?

Dillinger seemed to get even crazier the deeper they got into the Glades. Did Nick risk Vince, Brandi and Kody in the hope of saving a child who might be dead already by now?

"Help!"

He was startled to hear someone calling out weakly.

"Hey…for the love of God, help me. Please…"

The voice was barely a whisper. It was, however, Capone's voice.

"I hear him!" Vince said.

"Yeah, this way," Nick murmured.

He was startled when Vince suddenly grabbed him by the arm, so startled, he swung around with the Smith & Wesson he was carrying trained on the man.

"Whoa!" Vince said. "I guess you are one of them!"

"What?"

"You, uh, you've kept us alive a few times. I thought that maybe you were a good guy, but, hey…never mind."

Nick said nothing in response. He couldn't risk letting Vince in on the truth. The man talked too much. Instead, he turned, heading for the sound of Capone's weak voice.

Nick came upon him in a tangle of mangrove roots. Capone seemed to be caught beneath branches and roots that had actually tangled together.

"We thought a gator got you," Vince said.

"Gator? That Nelson is an idiot!" Capone said. "The branch broke, splashed down and pinned me here like a sitting duck. If there is some kind of major predator around… " He paused, looking up at Nick. "My leg is broken. I won't be able to make it to…wherever it is exactly that Dillinger wants to go. You gotta help me somehow, Barrow. You gotta help me. He'll kill me if I'm useless. Dillinger will kill me!"

Nick hesitated but Vince didn't.

"No, no, he likes you!" Vince said. "He just shot that other guy—Nelson—for leaving you!"

"He shot Nelson?" Capone demanded, staring at Nick.

"Yeah," Nick said quietly.

He reached down. First things first. He had to get Capone out of the mire he was tangled in.

There was a sudden fluttering sound as Nick lifted a heavy branch off the man. He had disturbed a flock of egrets, he saw. A loud buzzing sounded; he'd also attracted a nice swarm of mosquitos.

Vince swore, slapping at himself.

"Help me!" Nick snapped.

Vince went to work, slapping at his neck as he did so. "Amazing. Amazing that people actually came and stayed to live in these swamps."

He rambled on but Nick tuned him out. He was too busy detangling Capone.

When they lifted off the last branch and pile of brush, Capone let out a pained cry.

"My leg," he wailed. He looked at Nick desperately. "What the hell do I do? He'll kill me. No, no, we have to kill him, Nick. We have to kill him before he kills all of us."

"We can't just kill him, Capone," Nick said.

"Why the hell not? The hostages are free or with us. Once we kill him—"

"We don't know who he has coming. He made plans for this. Someone is bringing an airboat here. We're stuck, if you haven't noticed. And this may be a national park, but if you've ever spent any time in the Everglades, you know that we could be somewhere where no one will ever find us."

"We have guns."

"And he's got a kid stashed somewhere, too, Capone. A little kid."

"I know. He made sure we all knew. I'm sorry about the kid but—"

"I won't tell him that you wanted to kill him," Nick said firmly.

Capone stared at him and nodded.

"Yeah. Okay. But you watch. He's going to want to kill me."

"I can see that you're left behind. On the boat. The one we stole from that poor old man. Someone will come upon it eventually," Nick said.

"You can make that happen?"

Nick shrugged. "I can try. If you stay behind, it'll probably be the cops who find you. But, hey, these guys might speak nicely for you when it comes to sentencing."

Capone suddenly pulled back and shot him a look. "You're a cop!"

Nick didn't miss a beat. "I swear I am not a cop." Without a moment's hesitation he called to Vince for help lifting Capone.

With Capone shrieking in pain, they got the man up on his one good leg.

Just as they did, they heard the whirr of an airboat and saw a blinding light flood the area.

Sleeping birds shrieked and fluttered and rose high in flight.

Nick noticed the glassy eyes of a number of nearby gators; they'd been hidden in the darkness.

The sound of one engine sputtered and stopped; a second did so just a moment after.

Two airboats had arrived.

"Hey, are you having trouble?" someone shouted.

Nick couldn't see a thing; he was blinded.

But he didn't have to. He knew this had to be Dillinger's associate, whoever he had been waiting for to bring him the airboat.

"Broken leg!" Nick shouted.

The light seemed to lower. He saw the first airboat and a second airboat in back.

A man jumped off the first one and came sloshing through the water. He was quickly followed by another. Both men were tall and muscular and quick to help support Capone.

"Where's Dillinger?" the older of the two, a man with dark graying hair and a mustache and beard to match, asked Nick.

"Back at the boat we took this afternoon," Nick said.

"Cops have been looking for that ever since the old man who owned her got picked up by a Coast Guard vessel about an hour ago."

"You gotta ditch it," the younger man said. He looked just like the older man.

Father and son, Nick figured.

"Everyone is all right?" the older one asked, sounding nervous.

"Do I look all right?" Capone moaned.

"I meant..."

"The hostages are all alive. We've had a few difficulties," Nick said. "There—ahead, there's the boat!"

"Dillinger!"

Dillinger looked over the bow as Nick, Vince, Capone and the two unnamed newcomers came along, nearing the boat.

"Capone!" Dillinger cried. "I knew it. I just knew you weren't dead. You're too damned mean for any alligator to eat!" He frowned then, realizing how heavily Capone leaned upon the men at his sides. "What happened?" he asked darkly.

"We've brought you an airboat—just as you asked," the older of the men shouted.

"Good. How will you get back?" Dillinger asked.

"We've got a second boat. We'll get out of here and back to our business," the older man said.

"All right, go."

"We're even then, right?" the older man demanded. "We did what you wanted."

"Yep. You did what I wanted. Head to the old cemetery in the Grove. Find the grave of Daniel Paul Allegro. Dig at the foot. You'll find what you want. You've evened the score enough, so go," Dillinger said.

"How do I know that the papers are there?" the older man asked.

"You're going to have to trust me. But I've always been good to my word," Dillinger said.

The man with the graying dark hair and beard looked at Nick. "If you would help us...?"

"Yes, of course," Nick said. He took Capone's arm and wrapped it around his shoulder. The night was cool but Capone was still sweating profusely.

The men who had brought the airboat nodded and walked away.

Nick watched as they left, water splashing around them as they returned to the second airboat.

They'd owed Dillinger; he'd been holding something over them. Now all they wanted was to get away as quickly as possible, get to a graveyard and dig something up.

What hold could Dillinger have had on the men?

It didn't matter at the moment. What mattered was the fact that one man was dead and Capone couldn't move an inch on his own.

"My leg is broken!" Capone shouted up to Dillinger. "I'm in bad shape. I tripped, fell, Nelson went running off..."

Dillinger started swearing. "We've got to get you up here." He paced the deck, grabbing his head, swearing. "Floyd! Floyd, get up here, help!"

Floyd appeared on deck, looking around anxiously. He saw Capone. "Hey, you're alive!"

"Well, somewhat," Capone said.

It wasn't easy, but with help from Floyd and Vince, they got Capone onto the boat.

Nick crawled over the hull.

By then, Kody and Brandi had pillows and sheets taken from the boat's cabin stretched out and ready on the deck. In a few minutes, they had Capone comfortably situated. Vince had noted a broken plank caught up in a nearby mangrove. He hurried to get it and, between them all, they splinted Capone's leg.

"He needs medical care," Kody said.

"He can't go slogging through the Everglades, up on the hammocks, through the saw grass and the wetlands," Nick agreed quietly.

"I'll make it! I'll make whatever!" Capone said. "Don't…don't…"

"He thinks you're going to kill him," Vince told Dillinger.

"What?" Dillinger asked. He truly looked surprised.

"I'm like a lame horse," Capone said quietly.

Kody had been kneeling on the deck by him. She stood, retreated down the steps for a minute, and came back with a bottle of vodka.

"This will help," she said.

"I killed Nelson for leaving you, because we don't turn on each other," Dillinger said. He looked at his friend and reassured him.

"Then you have to leave me," Capone said, looking at Dillinger and taking a long swig of the vodka. He sighed softly, easing back as the alcohol eased some of his pain. "I swear there's nothing I will tell them. There's nothing I can tell them. I don't even know where you're going. Just leave me."

"You'll do time. You know you'll do time," Dillinger told him.

"Yes, yes, I will. But I may live long enough to get out," he said. "If I try to go with you…"

Dillinger thought about his words. He lowered his head. After a long moment he nodded.

He walked over to the big man on the ground, leaned down and embraced him.

Then he jerked up, his gun trained on the others.

"He stays. We go," he said.

Nick was startled when Kody spoke up. "You can't leave him, not like this."

"Miss Cameron," Nick said, trying to step in, trying to stop whatever bad things her words might do to Dillinger's mind.

"He needs help. Look," Kody said, determined. "Brandi is screaming and scared and freaking us all out. She needs to be picked up as soon as possible. And Capone here needs help. Leave the two of them. Capone still has his gun, and Brandi isn't a cruel person. They have enough supplies on the boat to get them through the night okay. I say we leave them both." She turned to Dillinger. "That leaves five of us. Five of us in good health and good shape and not prone to hysterics in any way. We can make it."

Dillinger stared back at her. Nick barely dared to breathe.

Dillinger smiled. "You are quite something, Miss Cameron. I think you might have something. All right! Get supplies together. We leave Capone and little Miss Cry Baby here. Actually, Blondie, you really were starting to get on my nerves. Let's do it."

"You want to move deep into the Everglades by night?" Vince asked Dillinger.

"Well, hell, yes, of course!" Dillinger said. "The cops or someone will be around here very soon. We've got to get deep into the swamp and the muck and the hell of it all before the law comes around. Darkness, my boy! Yes, great. Into the abyss! Indeed, into the abyss!"

Chapter Six

The airboat was a flat-bottomed, aluminum-and-fiberglass craft with the engine and propeller held in a giant metal cage at the rear. Dillinger prodded everyone in.

Kody recalled the two men who had come to deliver the boat. They hadn't looked like bad men.

Once again she asked herself, *So what did bad men look like?*

Why didn't Barrow look like a bad man? Was he a good man—somehow under the influence of real criminals because he was between a rock and a hard place? He had a child somewhere being held, perhaps. Somehow, he was being coerced…either that, or she was simply being really drawn to someone really, really bad—and she couldn't accept that!

She had a hard time understanding what was going on with any of the men. She wished she could close her eyes and open them to find out that everything that had happened had occurred in her imagination.

But it was real. Too real.

At least she was grateful that Dillinger had listened to her and left both Capone and Brandi behind.

Alive.

As she was. For now…

Amid the deafening sounds of the motors she looked out into the night.

It was dark. Darker than any darkness Kody had ever known before. There was a haze before her to the north, and she knew the haze she saw was the light that illuminated the city of Miami and beyond up the coast.

But it was far away.

Out here Kody had no concept of time. She realized suddenly that she was tired, exhausted. It had to be getting close to the middle of the night. It seemed they'd been moving forever, but, of course, out here, that didn't mean much. Unless you were a ranger or a native of the area, each canal, new hammock and twist and zig or zag of the waterways seemed the same. The glow of gator eyes—caught by the headlights of the airboat—was truly chilling.

And despite it all, she'd nearly drifted to sleep twice. Vince had caught her both times.

Suddenly the whirr of the airboat stopped. She jerked awake—as did Vince at her side.

"Where are we?" Vince murmured.

Kody didn't know. But as she blinked in the darkness, Barrow and Floyd jumped out of the airboat and caught hold of the hull, pulling it—with the others still aboard—up on a hammock of higher, dry land. The lights still shone for a moment, long enough for Kody to see there was a chickee hut before them. It was the kind of abode the Seminole and Miccosukee tribes of Florida had learned to use years before—built up off the ground, open to allow for any breeze, and covered with the palms and fronds that were so abundant.

She was still staring blankly at the chickee hut when she realized Barrow had come back to the airboat—and that he had a hand out to assist her from her chair.

She was so tired that she didn't think; she accepted his hand. And she was so tired that she slipped coming off the airboat.

He swept her up quickly. Instinctively she wound her arms around his neck.

It felt right; it felt good to hold on to him…

She wanted to cry out and pull away. And she didn't know why she felt with such certainty that he would protect her and that he'd keep her from harm.

He set her down on dry ground. "Hop on up. I'm going to light a fire," he said, indicating the chickee hut.

It was just a few feet off the ground. Vince was already there. He offered her an assist up and she took it.

There was nothing in the little hut—nothing at all. But it was dry and safe, Kody thought. Floyd was up on the platform with them and he indicated that the two of them should sit. "Make yourselves as comfortable as you can. Grab what sleep you can. This isn't exactly the Waldorf but…"

Kody took a seat in the rear of the chickee hut and Vince followed her. She could hear Dillinger and Barrow talking, but they kept their argument low and nothing of it could be heard.

Vince shook his head. "What the hell?" he murmured.

Kody reached for his hand and squeezed it. "Hey. We're going to be okay."

"Yeah."

"Just follow directions and you'll be okay," Floyd said.

They were both silent. Then Vince spoke, as if he just had to have something to fill the silence of the night.

"Did you know that Alexander Graham Bell led the team that created the first airboat?" Vince asked idly as they sat there. "And it was up in Nova Scotia? The thing was called the *Ugly Duckling*. Cool, huh? The things are useful down here—and on ice for rescues. Go figure."

"Sure, cool," Kody agreed. "I had not known that," she said lightly.

"Alexander Graham Bell, huh, go figure!" Floyd said.

Kody thought Floyd was just as interested in what the others were saying as she and Vince were. He kept trying to listen. He had his gun on his lap—ready to grab up—but Kody was getting a different feeling from the man than she had earlier. Somehow, right now, he didn't seem as dangerous.

Floyd inched closer. "Do you really think you can find this treasure stash Dillinger thinks you can find?" he asked, looking first at Kody and then on to Vince. "I guess I never knew the guy. I mean, I hope you can find that treasure. Seems like the only one who can kind of keep Dillinger in check right now is Barrow, but even then…" His voice trailed. He squinted—as if squinting might make him hear more clearly.

Kody glanced at Vince and then at Floyd. "I don't know. I mean…we're following a written trail. Things change. The land out here changes, too." She hesitated and then asked, "Do you think he's going to kill us all?"

Floyd shrugged. "Hell, I don't know. I actually wish I was Capone! Yeah, they'll get him. Yeah, he'll go to jail. But he won't die out here in this godforsaken swamp!"

"Why don't you just shoot him?" Vince asked. "You just shoot Dillinger dead when he least expects it. Kody and I disappear until we can get help. You disappear into the world somewhere, too. You don't want to hurt us, and we won't turn you in. The three of us—we live."

Floyd hesitated, looking away. "Dillinger won't do it—he, um, he won't kill us."

"He might! Why take a chance?" Vince said.

Floyd smiled. "Don't kid yourself. I could never outdraw Barrow. I could never even take him by surprise." He lifted his shoulders in a hunch and then let them fall. "If I could…no. You've got to be careful, toe the line! Barrow is freaked out that Dillinger kidnapped that kid. Barrow can't take the kid thing and I think he's pretty sure the boy is stashed somewhere and he'll wind up dying if we don't get the truth from Dillinger. He won't do anything until Dillinger gives up the kid, and now that we're out here… I don't know how in hell that's going to happen."

Kody swatted hard at an insect, her mind racing. "If

the police just got their hands on Dillinger, they could make him talk."

Floyd shook his head. "Dillinger's real name is Nathan Appleby. I'm not supposed to know any of this. None of us is supposed to know about the others. But I was at this place Dillinger was staying at in the Grove one day and I found some of his papers and then I looked up anything I could about him. He served fifteen years of a life sentence up north. He and some other guys had kidnapped a white-collar executive. He wouldn't give up the guys he was working with to the cops—or the old crack house where they were holding their hostage. The hostage wound up dying of an overdose shot up into his veins by the people holding him. Nathan's gang on that one did get away with the money. But one of them betrayed Nathan. That guy wound up in the Hudson River.

"See, that's just it—he holds things over on people. Like the guys who brought the airboat. He had papers on them, I'm willing to bet, which would have proven the older man's—the dad's, I'm pretty sure—illegal status here in the USA. And, I'm willing to bet, when Nathan gets what he wants here, he's got some other poor idiot he's blackmailing somehow to have a mode of transportation available for him that will get him out of the country. Not so hard from here, you know. He can get to the Bahamas or Cuba damned easily, and move on from there."

Kody had been so intent on Floyd's words that she didn't hear or see Dillinger approaching until Vince nudged her. She turned to see that Dillinger and Barrow had come up on the platform. She wasn't sure if Dillinger had heard what Floyd had been saying.

"What's going on here?" Dillinger asked.

"I'm telling them that they'd be crazy to try to escape," Floyd said. "Nowhere to go."

"I don't believe you," Dillinger said. There was ice in his voice. He raised his gun.

Kody wasn't sure what might have happened if she hadn't moved, and she wasn't the least sure of what she was doing.

She was just very afraid that Dillinger was about to shoot Floyd.

She rolled off the ledge of the chickee hut and landed down on the ground of the little hardwood hammock they had come upon.

And she began to run.

He wouldn't fire at her, would he? Dillinger wouldn't fire at her!

She heard a shot. It was a warning shot, she knew. It went far over her head.

And she stopped running. She couldn't see anything at all, except for large shadowlike things in the night, created by the weak moonlight that filtered through here and there. She tried to turn and her foot went into some kind of a mud hole. She stood for a moment, breathing deeply, wondering what the hell she had done—and what the hell she could do now.

She could hide and maybe they wouldn't find her.

"Kody."

She heard her name spoken softly. It was Barrow. She turned but she couldn't see him.

"Stay where you are," he whispered. "Don't move."

She stood still, puzzled, afraid—and lost.

And then she understood. At first it sounded as if she was hearing pigs rooting around in a sty. Then she realized the sound was a little different.

She felt Barrow's hand on her upper arm, at the same time gentle and firm. He jerked her back, playing a light over the muck she'd just stepped into.

And right there in the mud hole she saw a good-size group of alligators. They weren't particularly big, but there were plenty of them gathered together on the surface of the mud.

She froze and her breath stalled in her throat.

"Come on!" he said, pulling her away.

With his urging, she managed to move back. She realized she had come fairly far—the chickee hut and the fire Barrow had built were a distance ahead through a maze of brush and trees. She knew then that this was the opportunity she'd been waiting for. She turned to Barrow.

"He's going to kill everyone and you know it," Kody said.

"I don't intend to let him kill everyone," he said. "You have to believe me."

He looked directly into her eyes then and, in the light of the flashlight, she saw his face clearly. She wasn't sure why, but at that moment she remembered where and when she had seen Barrow before.

In New York City. She and Kevin had been walking out of Finnegan's. He'd been telling her that he had a secret new love in his life, and he was very excited.

And she had been laughing and telling him she was glad she was all into her career and the move to New York, because she didn't have anyone who resembled a love—new or old—in her life at all.

And that's when she'd plowed into him. Run right into him. He'd been there with another man—Craig Frasier. Of course, she knew Craig Frasier because she knew his girlfriend Kieran Finnegan.

They paused to look at one another, both apologizing and then…

She'd thought instantly that he felt great, smelled great, had a wonderful smile, and that she wanted to find out more about him. She'd hoped he wasn't married, engaged or dating, that she'd be able to see him and…

Then Kevin had grasped her arm and they'd hurried on out and…

Her mind whirled as the memories assailed her.

"You're FBI!" she said.

His hand on her arm tensed and he pulled her closer. "Shh!"

"All along, you're FBI. You could have shot him dead several times now. We're here, out in the true wilds, the Everglades where even the naturalists and the Native Americans and park rangers don't come! You could have shot him, you—"

"Shh! Please!"

"You didn't say anything to me! Not a word," Kody told him. She was shaking, furiously—and still scared as could be.

"I couldn't risk it," he said.

"But I recognize you—"

"It took you a while," he said. "Look, if you'd recognized me and it had shown, and Dillinger had known, or Schultz, or even one of the others, we could all be dead now. I just infiltrated this gang not long ago. It should have been easy enough. We should have gotten into the house. I should have been able to design a way in for the cops and the FBI, but…there's a little boy out there. Dillinger kidnapped a kid. I have to get him to tell me where he's holding that boy."

She stared at him, sensing his dilemma, because she herself felt torn.

On the one hand, her desire to survive was strong.

And on the other hand, she couldn't let an innocent child die.

"You've had opportunities to tell me," she said. "I could maybe help."

"How?"

"You're forgetting—he believes he needs me. He thinks I know all about Anthony Green and the stash of riches from the bank heist Green pulled off years and years ago. Maybe he'll talk to me. Maybe he will—you don't know!"

"And maybe he won't. And maybe he'll figure out that Vince is really more up on history than you are and that he needs him—and doesn't need you. Dammit, I'm trying to keep everyone alive," Barrow said to her.

Barrow. His real name was Nick. Nicholas Connolly. Now she remembered clear as day.

She remembered everything. She'd asked Kieran

and Craig about him later, and they'd told her his name—and what he did!

"You're on some kind of a team with Craig Frasier. He's the one you've been talking to all along on the negotiations," Kody said.

"A task force. And, yes. Our task force has followed Dillinger—actually, Nathan Appleby—from New York on down. And now…we've got to stop him here. But we've seen what he's capable of. We have to find that boy before Nathan knows that he's trapped." He was staring at her and he let out a long breath.

"What do we do?" she whispered. "He's—he's crazy. Even Floyd thinks he's crazy. He shot and killed one of his own men!"

"We go back. We make it through the night," he told her. "There's nowhere to go out here. We're north of the tip of the peninsula and south of Tamiami Trail and the Shark Valley entrance up that way. A mile here is like a hundred miles somewhere else. The chickee is the safest place to be for the night." When she shivered, he added, "One of us will be on guard through the darkness."

She looked at him.

He was right about one thing.

She didn't want to just walk into the darkness of the Everglades.

Vipers, constrictors and crocodilians, oh, my.

"Okay," Kody said quietly. "Okay. So we go back. Morning comes. We head to what I believe to be the area where Anthony Green had his distillery, his Everglades hideout. And what happens if I can't find the treasure he wants? What happens if you can't find the boy?"

"I have to believe that we'll get what we need—that somewhere in all this, Dillinger will trust me and that I can get him talking. And if not, I pray that the cops and the FBI and everyone else working the kid's disappearance will find a clue. One way or the other, I will see to it that you and your friend, Vince, are safe by tomorrow morning. I got information to Craig. They know where to go. They'll have a very carefully laid ambush for tomorrow. We just have to get to that time."

Kody nodded dully. Okay. She'd go back.

He suddenly pulled her into his arms; she swallowed hard, looking up at him, seeing the emotion conflicting in his eyes.

"I'll keep you safe!" he vowed. "I'll keep you safe!"

"I know!" she whispered, hoping there was more courage in her voice than she felt.

"I have to make this look real," he told her.

She felt the muzzle of his gun against her back. "Of course."

Dillinger was standing by the edge of the chickee hut ledge when they returned—watching for them.

"My dear Miss Cameron! Foolish girl. Where were you going to go?" he asked.

"She's not going anywhere. She's going to be by my side from here on out," Barrow—or, rather, Nick Connolly—told him.

"Let's hope not. It's getting late. We could all use a little sleep. Oh, but, please, don't go thinking that my fellows are sweet on you, Miss Cameron, or that if I sleep, you can run again," Dillinger said. "I wake at a whisper in the wind. You will not pull things over on me.

"Not to mention…the coral snake doesn't have much of a mouth span, but the bite can be lethal. There are pygmy rattlers out there and Eastern diamondbacks. And the cottonmouth. Nasty, all of them. Not to mention the pythons and boas. But, since I'm being honest here, I haven't heard of anyone being snuffed out by one of them yet. There are the alligators and the crocs—mostly alligators where we are right now, but, hey, if you're going to get mauled or eaten by an alligator or a croc, do you really care which one?"

"I'm not going anywhere," Kody said. "You scared me. You scared me worse than the thought of a snake or an alligator or whatever else might be out here." She inhaled air as if she could breathe in courage. So far, it seemed to work with him. "You have to stop. You got mad at your own man for nothing. You—you shot one of your own men."

"He betrayed the brotherhood," Dillinger said.

"I want us all to live. You want Vince and me to find your treasure. So quit scaring everyone so much and we'll find your treasure."

Dillinger smiled and glanced at Barrow where he stood right behind her.

"This one is a little firecracker, isn't she?" Dillinger asked.

"And you need her," Barrow said softly. "And you do have your code of honor, Dillinger. None of these people has betrayed anyone, so let's just let them be.

Meanwhile it's you, me and Floyd taking turns on guard. We'll get some sleep."

"Sure," he said. "Floyd, there's some water and some kind of food bars on the airboat. Go get 'em."

"On it, boss," Floyd said.

Kody realized that she was desperately parched for water—and that she was starving, too.

Barrow—Nick—walked around her, leaped up onto the platform and then reached a hand down to help her up.

She accepted it.

And when Floyd came with the water and power bars, she gratefully accepted those, as well.

After she ate, she found herself curling into a little ball on the wooden platform. Vince was to her one side. Nick was to her other side, leaning against one of the support poles.

"I'll take the first hours," Dillinger said. "Floyd, you're up next."

Hours later, Kody realized she had fallen asleep. She opened her eyes and Nick was still by her side, sitting close beside her, awake, keeping guard. She could feel his warmth, he was so close, and it was good.

The night had been cold, and she was scared, but she'd slept, knowing Nick Connolly remained at her side.

She looked up at him. His eyes were open and he was watching her. She was startled to feel a flood of warmth streak through her.

Of course, she remembered now when she had initially met him. Her reaction had been quite a normal one for a woman meeting such a striking man. He was really attractive with his fit build and dark blue, intense eyes. She'd had to hurry out that night at Finnegan's, but she'd thought that maybe she'd see him again.

Then life, work and other things had intervened.

And now…

He was good, she thought. Good at what he did. He had kept all the hostages alive so far. He had gotten many of them to safety.

He was still a very attractive man. Even covered in Everglades' mud and muck. With his broad shoulders and muscled arms he looked like security. Strength. And she was so tempted to draw closer to him, to step into the safe haven of those arms…

What was she thinking? This had to be some kind of syndrome, she told herself. Kieran Finnegan would be able to explain it to her. It was a syndrome wherein women fell in love with their captors.

No, she wasn't in love. And he wasn't really a captor. He was as G-man and he worked with Craig Frasier!

"You okay?" he whispered.

She nodded.

"I will get you out of this."

"Yes…I believe you."

He nodded grimly.

"Vince? Is Vince all right."

"Right now? He's quite all right. Take a look."

Kody rolled carefully to take a look at Vince. He was actually snoring softly.

She turned back to Nick. She nodded and offered him a small, grim smile.

"Hey! You're up, Barrow!" Dillinger suddenly called out.

"Yep, I'm on it," Nick called back to him.

He stood. Kody saw that he'd never let go of his gun, that it was held tightly in his hands.

It would be so easy! So easy for Nick just to walk over and shoot the man who was holding them all hostage, threatening their lives.

But she saw the way that Dillinger was sleeping. His gun in his lap.

The man even slept with his damned eyes open!

Kody didn't sleep again. She watched as the sun came up. It was oddly beautiful. The colors that streaked the sky were magnificent. Herons and cranes, white and colorful, flew to the water's edge. Then nature called.

She stood and saw that Floyd and Dillinger and Nick were all up. Nick had gone over to kick the fire out. There was little preparation to be made for them to move on, but they were obviously ready to go.

She cleared her throat.

"I...I need a few moments alone," Kody said. "I need privacy."

"Don't we all," Dillinger said.

"I'm serious. I need to take a little walk. As you've pointed out, there's really nowhere for me to go. I insist. I mean it, or you can shoot me now!"

Dillinger started to laugh. "Okay, Barrow, take Miss Cameron down a path. Give her some space—but not too much. You seem to be good at hunting her down, but we're ready to move on and I don't want to waste any time."

"Yeah, fine," Nick said.

"Don't worry. Hey, I'm fine right here!" Vince said. "It's a guy thing, right? No one cares about my privacy, huh?"

They all ignored Vince.

"Go. Move! There's a trail there," Nick told her.

She walked ahead of him, aware that Dillinger was watching. Nick kept his gun trained on her.

A great blue heron stood in her way. The bird looked at her a moment and then lifted into flight. It was beautiful…and it was all so wrong.

Fifty feet out and into the trees, she turned and told Nick, "I really need privacy. I won't go anywhere, I swear."

"Scream bloody murder if you need me," he said and stopped.

She'd really only need a few seconds—what they used to call *necessary* seconds for the nonexistent facilities out here—but she was one of those people who absolutely needed to be alone.

The hammock was riddled with what they called gator holes—little areas of mud and muck dug out by gators when they tried to cool themselves off in summer. It was winter now, but the holes remained. One was full of water and she dared dip her hands in, anxious to pretend she was dealing with something that resembled normalcy and hygiene.

She looked up, ready to rise—and a scream caught in her throat.

She was staring at a man. He had coal-dark eyes and long dark braids, and he was dressed in greenish-brown khaki jeans and a cotton shirt. He was, she knew, either Miccosukee or Seminole, and he was capable of being as silent as a whisper in the air.

He quickly showed her a badge and brought his finger to his lips. "Tell Nick that Jason Tiger is here," he said softly. Then he disappeared back into the brush by the gator hole.

He might never have been there.

Chapter Seven

"Jason Tiger," Kody said, whispering as she returned to Nick. "He showed me his badge!"

Instead of taking her by the arm to lead her back, Nick reached down and pretended to tie his shoes. "Tiger?" he said. He didn't know why he needed the affirmation. If Kody had said the name, she had certainly seen the man.

His heart skipped a beat.

He silently sent up a little prayer of thanks.

He'd known Jason Tiger from years before, when they'd both attended the same Florida state university. Neither of them had been FBI then. Since then he'd seen Jason only once, just briefly, right before he'd gone undercover.

The name Tiger signified one of the dominant clans of the Miccosukee. Jason had been proud to tell him that his family clan was that of William Buffalo Tiger, who was just recently deceased, and had been the first elected tribal chairman when the Miccosukee had been recognized as a tribe in the 1960s. Jason knew the Everglades as few others. He'd been recognized by the

FBI for the contributions he'd made in bringing down murderers and drug lords—those who had used what Jason considered to be the precious beauty and diversity of the Everglades to promote their criminal activities.

If Kody had seen Jason Tiger, they were going to be all right.

Jason would be reporting to Craig and the county police and the tribal police and every other law enforcement officer out there.

It was good.

It was more than good; it was a tremendous relief. Jason was out there and Nick wasn't working this alone anymore.

He stood and grabbed her arm. "All right." He nodded, knowing that was all the reassurance he could give her right now. Just fifty feet away, he felt Dillinger looking their way.

He held her arm tighter as they returned to the chickee. He couldn't show the relief he was feeling. He didn't dare defy Dillinger as yet—not until they knew the whereabouts of the boy. And still, the lives of Kody and Vince were at stake.

Kody wrenched free from his hold as they neared the airboat. He wasn't prepared. She managed the feat easily.

She walked over to Dillinger. He followed closely, ready to intervene.

"I don't care about the money or your treasure or whatever," she told him. "I'm more than willing to help you find it and you are just welcome to it. But if you want my help—or Vince's help—you better tell us where that little boy is. You kidnapped a kid. We've been out overnight now. That little boy is somewhere terrified, I imagine. Let him go, and I will dig from here until eternity to find the treasure for you."

Nick realized he was holding his breath, standing as tense as steel—and ready to draw on Dillinger or throw himself in front of Kody Cameron.

But Dillinger laughed softly.

He stared at Kody, obviously amused. "Wow. Hey, Vince, is that true? You don't care about yourself, right? You'll work yourself to the bone for me—if I tell you where the kid is, right? Yeah, Vince, you ready to throw your own life away for a kid you've never seen?"

Vince didn't answer. He pushed his glasses up the bridge of his nose, looking nervous.

"Okay, Miss Cameron, you want to know where the kid is? He's up in the northwest area, an abandoned crack house that's ridiculously close to the fancy new theater they've got up there north of the stadium. So, there's your kid. Yeah, it's probably getting bad for him. He was a pain in the ass, you know. I had to tie him up and stuff a gag in his mouth. So, I'm going to suggest you find this treasure for me as quickly as possible. Then I'll leave you where—if you're lucky—some kind of cop will find you before the wildlife does. And you can tell the cops where to look. You happy now?"

For a moment the air seemed to ring with his words. And then everyone and everything was silent, down to the insects.

"Yes, thank you!" Kody snapped at last, and she hurried past Dillinger, ready to hop aboard the airboat.

Dillinger studied Nick for a long moment. Nick was afraid he was on to something.

Then Dillinger smiled. "I will get what I want!" he said softly.

"I'm sure you will. I have to tell you, I'm confused. What the hell is the idea with the boy? I mean, we're in the Everglades. The boy is in an abandoned crack house."

"If they find us—not an impossible feat, even out here—I may need to use that boy to get free," Dillinger said.

"You have hostages."

"And by the time we find the treasure, we may not," Dillinger said. He shook his head, swearing. "Here we are, end of the road, the prize in sight. And I'm down at the finish line with you and Floyd, the two most squeamish crooks I've come across in a long career."

"I told you, I'm not in this to kill people. I never was. I like the finer things in life. I've been around, too. You can survive without killing people," Nick said. "I'm also against the jail terms or the needle that can come with killing people."

"Ah, well, they can only stick a needle in once," Dillinger said. "And we've already killed people, haven't we?"

"You killed Nelson. I sure as hell had no part in that. The hostages… Thanks to me, we're not going to die because of them."

"Ah, but you did kill Schultz, didn't you?" Dillinger

accused him. "It's so obvious, my friend. You've got a thing for the woman. Schultz was getting too close. You took care of him, huh?" Barrow asked, his grin broad—eerie and frightening—as he stared at Nick.

And Nick was good at this, the mind game—delving into the psyche of criminals, following the trails of sick minds.

But he wasn't sure about Dillinger. Nick had studied this man. But, right now, he wasn't sure.

"You'll never really know, will you?" he asked Dillinger quietly, and he was pleased to see a worried frown crease the man's brow. Dillinger didn't know; the man really didn't know if Barrow would go ballistic on him or not.

Pull a trigger—or not.

It was good. It was very good to keep Dillinger off guard.

"Thing is, no one has any idea who killed old Schultz. You shot Nelson in front of the hostages. Oh, yeah, so you don't intend that Dakota and the young man should live, right? Well, start thinking anew. I'll help make sure you get the hell out of here. But you aren't killing that girl. You've got it right. I've got a thing for her. And she's coming with me."

"And then what, you idiot?" Dillinger demanded angrily. "You're going to just keep her? Keep her alive? You will rot in jail, you idiot."

"You'll be long gone—what will you care?"

"She'd better find what I want, that's all I've got to say. You want her alive? She'd better find it."

Nick looked at the ground and then shook his head

as he looked back up at Dillinger. "You want to know if I can be a killer? Touch a hair on her head. You'll find out."

"Really?" Dillinger said, intrigued.

"Yeah. Really."

With that he shoved his way past Dillinger and headed toward the airboat.

In minutes, it seemed that they indeed flew, the craft moving swiftly across the shallow water and marshes of the Everglades.

"SUCH AN INTERESTING PLACE," Dillinger said, "this 'River of Grass!' If one wants to be poetic, I mean. Imagine Anthony Green. Out here, in pretty good shape. But he's out of ammunition and there are a dozen deadly creatures you can encounter in every direction—with no real defense. Imagine being here. Deserted. Alone. With nothing."

Kody didn't answer him or even respond, even though Vince looked at her nervously, apparently praying she had some clue as to what they were doing.

They'd traveled for hours until she'd told them to stop. Now she held a map unfolded from the back page of one of the journals. She pointed in what she truly hoped was the right direction. "Anthony Green's illegal liquor operation was out here, right on this hammock. When he had the place, he had workstations set up—chickees. But there was a main chickee where he set up a desk and papers and did his bookkeeping."

"Obviously, not here anymore, right?" Dillinger asked, eyes narrowed as he stared at her.

"You're sure this is the right place?" Floyd asked her.

"I'm not *sure* of anything," Kody said. "I know that there were four chickees and all the parts for having a distillery. I'm thinking that they were set about the hammock in a square formation, with the 'cooking' going on right in the middle by the water. Remember, land floods and land washes away. But I do think that we have the right hammock area..." She paused and looked over at Vince. "Right?"

"The Everglades is full of hammocks," Vince murmured. "Hardwood hammocks, with gumbo limbo trees, mahogany and more, and there are pine islands. Unless you really know the Everglades, it can all be the same."

"My sense of direction isn't great," Kody said. "But I believe that we did follow the known byways from the southern entrance to the park and that, if we were to continue to the north, we would come upon Shark Valley and Tamiami Trail. Naturally, we've really got to hope that this was the hammock. But—"

"Great," Floyd murmured. "We have to hope!"

Kody ignored him. "Okay, so, the heating source they used was fire, but anything they might have used to create fire would have been swallowed up long ago into nature. But Green had a massive stainless-steel still and a smaller copper still—a present to Green from the real Al Capone—and other tools that were made of copper or stainless steel. If we can find even the remnants of any of the containers, we'll know we're in the right place."

"This is ridiculous," Floyd told Dillinger. "Even if

we find a piece of stainless steel, how are we going to find out where the chickees were? This has been an idiot's quest from the get-go, Dillinger!"

The way Dillinger looked at Floyd was frightening.

Floyd quickly realized his mistake and lifted a hand. "Sorry, man. I just don't see how we're going to find this."

"There is hope," Kody said quickly. "There are notes in Anthony Green's journal about his chickees. He didn't intend that his operations be washed away in a storm. Each one of the chickees was built with pilings that went deep into the earth. If we see any sign of pilings or of the remnants of a still, we'll know we're in the right place."

"Well, we know what we need to do." Nick stepped forward, defusing the tension and getting the group to focus on the task at hand. "We need to all start looking. Span out over the hammock, but be careful. There are snakes that like to hide in the tall grasses. Vince and Kody, you stay to the center and see if you can find remnants of a still. Floyd, you and Dillinger, try the upper left quadrant over there. I'll head to the right. We're looking for any one of the sections where the workmen's chickees might have stood."

It was like looking for a needle in a haystack. Time passed. Decades. There were so few of them; there was so much ground to cover.

"Let's cover each other, crossing positions around here," Vince suggested to Kody.

She looked at him, smiled and nodded. He was a good guy, she thought. Afraid, certainly, but doing his best to be courageous when it didn't look good at all for them.

Vince didn't know that "Barrow" was FBI. She longed to tell him but she wasn't sure if that would be wise. Vince could still panic, say something.

"We're going to be okay," she told him.

"Yeah. We're going to have to make a break for it somehow," he told her. "Do you realize that if we really find this stash—oh, so impossible!—Dillinger will kill us?"

"Maybe he'll let us go," Kody said.

"He killed one of his own men!"

"Yes, but that man deserted one of his friends. Maybe he does have some kind of criminal code of honor," Kody said.

Vince shook his head. "We have to get out of here," he said.

"But what is your suggestion on how?" Kody asked. "We're in the center. The three guys with guns can focus on us in a matter of seconds."

"Two of them won't kill us—neither Floyd nor Barrow," Vince said, his voice filled with certainty. "We just have to watch out for Dillinger."

"Who has an automatic weapon," Kody murmured. "We might be all right, Vince. Help will be on the way."

Vince let out a snort. "Yeah. Help. In the middle of the Everglades."

"Okay, so, to us it's a big swamp. But there are people who know it well, down to each mangrove tree, just about. It's going to be okay."

"Hey!" Dillinger suddenly called. "Are you two working out there?"

"Yes!" Kody shouted.

"Anything?" Nick asked.

Kody turned, hearing Nick's voice behind her. He was walking in quickly toward where they stood.

But before he could speak, Vince stood and stared at her, shaking his head, a look of desperation in his eyes. "We're going to die. If we just stay here, we're going to die. I'd rather feed a gator than take one of that asshole's bullets. I'm sorry, Kody."

He turned, ducking low into the high grasses, and began to run.

"What the hell?" Dillinger shouted.

He began to fire.

Nick threw himself on top of Kody, bringing her down to the damp, marshy earth. The gunfire continued and then stopped.

"Now, take my hand. Run!" Nick told her. He had her hand; he was pulling her. He came halfway to his feet and let go with a spray of bullets.

Then, hunched low, and all but dragging her behind him, he started to run.

Kody was stunned; she had no idea where they were going or why they had chosen that moment to leave. Vince had wanted to run…

Where was he?

Had he been shot?

What about Floyd? Was he shooting at them along with Dillinger?

Kody just knew that, for the moment, they were racing through a sea of grass and marsh. Her feet sank into mush with their every movement. Grass rose high around her, the saw grass tearing into her flesh here and there.

"Low! Keep low!" Nick told her.

Keep low and run? So difficult!

She could still hear Dillinger firing, but the sound was nowhere near as loud as it had been.

While Kody had no idea where they were running to, apparently Nick did. She felt the ground beneath her feet harden. They had come to a definite rise of high hammock ground, possibly a limestone shelf. She was gasping for breath and tugged back hard on Nick's hand.

"Breathe. Just breathe!" she gasped out.

And he stood still, pulling her against him as she dragged in breath after breath.

Suddenly the sound of gunfire stopped.

Now they could hear Dillinger shouting. "You're a dead man, Barrow! You're dead. I'll find you. And I'll let you watch me rip your pretty little pet to shreds before I kill you both. You're an ass. If the cops get you, you'll face a needle just like me!"

Nick remained still, just holding Kody.

"You can come back! You, too, Floyd! You can come back and we'll find the treasure, and we'll go on, free as the birds. I know where to go from here. I've got friends, you know that! They'll see that we get out of here safely. We can be sipping on silly drinks with umbrellas in them. Hey, come on now. Barrow, just bring her on back. I won't kill her, I promise. I just want that damned treasure!"

Nick held still and then brought his finger to his lips. He started to walk again—away from the sound of Dillinger ranting.

As they moved, though, they could still hear the man. "Vince! You idiot. Why did you run? I wouldn't have killed you. I just need the knowledge that you have. You're going to die out here. You have no way back in. I'm your way back in. Floyd! Oh, Floyd. You'd better be running. You are such a dead man. Such a namby-pamby dead man. I will find you. I will see that you die in agony, do you hear me? You are dead! You're all dead! I will find you!"

Only when Dillinger's voice had grown fainter did Kody dare to speak. "What the hell was that? What just happened? You said that a child would die. That—"

"Jason Tiger is out here," Nick said. "I'm going to get you to him as quickly as possible, and then I'll try to find your friend Vince."

"But the child. The little boy..."

"Adrian Burke," Nick said, smiling at her. He was studying her with a strange mixture of awe and disbelief. "Jason was still out there when we took off this morning. I met up with him earlier, looking for the pilings. Jason overheard Dillinger give up the boy's location. He got a message through to Craig Frasier and the local cops. They searched all the buildings in the area that Dillinger mentioned and they found the little boy. He's safe."

"Oh, my God! Really?" Kody asked. She wasn't

sure if she believed it herself. She was so relieved that she felt ridiculously weak—almost as if she would fall.

"They found him—because of me confronting Dillinger?" she asked incredulously.

"Yep." He looked uncomfortable for a minute. "I should have trusted you," he said softly. "I should have trusted in you earlier."

"I'm just—I'm just so grateful!"

"Me, too. The kids…finding kids. It's always the hardest!"

She was still standing God-alone-knew-where in the middle of deadly wilderness, and it would be wise not to fall. She blindly reached out. Nick caught her hands, steadying her.

"I have to get back around to where I can leave you with Jason Tiger," he told her. "Then I can look for your friend."

"There was so much gunfire," Kody said. "But Vince… Vince is smart. There's a chance he made it." She paused, as if to reassure herself, then said, "He was determined to escape. He was certain that Dillinger would have killed us."

Nick was quiet.

"He would have killed us," Kody said.

"Most likely. Come on. We're on solid ground here, and I think I know where I'm going, but I haven't worked down here in Florida for years."

"You worked here—in Florida?"

"I did. I'm from Florida."

"Ah. But…you know Craig?"

"I work in New York City now," he told her. "I

often work with him there. I've been on a task force with Craig and his partner. We've been following Dillinger—Nathan Appleby—all the way down the coast. I was the one who had never been seen, and I know the area, so I fit the bill to infiltrate. Especially once we knew that Dillinger was down here. That he was forming a gang and pulling off narcotic sales, prostitution, kidnapping…murder."

She was really shivering, she realized.

But it wasn't just fear. The sun was going down.

A South Florida winter was nothing like a northeastern winter, but here, on the water, with the sun going down, it was suddenly chilly. She was cold, teeth chattering, limbs quaking. And he was watching her with those eyes of his, holding her, and he seemed to be a bastion of heat and strength. She didn't want to lean on him so heavily. They were still in danger—very real, serious danger. And yet she felt ridiculously attracted to him. They'd both been hot, covered in swamp water, tinged with long grasses…

She was certain that, at the moment, her hair could best be described as stringy.

Her flesh was burned and scratched and raw…

And she was still breathing!

Was that it? She had survived. Nick had been a captor at first, and now he was a savior. Did all of that mess with the mind? Was she desperate to lean on the man because there was really something chemical and physical and real between them, or was she suffering some kind of mental break brought on by all that had happened?

She never got the chance to figure out which.

"Come on," he urged her.

And they began to move again, deep into the swamp. She felt his hand on hers. She felt a strange warmth sweeping through her.

Even as she shivered.

THEY WEREN'T IN a good position, but once Vince had suddenly decided to run, there had been no help for it.

Nick couldn't have gone after Vince and brought him down and go on pretending he was still part of Dillinger's plan. If he'd brought Vince back to Dillinger, the man would have killed Vince.

There had been nothing else to do but run then. Now all he could do was hope that Vince was smart enough to stay far, far away from Dillinger. And while Nick hadn't seen Floyd disappear, it was pretty clear from Dillinger's shouting that he'd used the opportunity to get away, as well.

It was one thing to be a criminal. It was another to be a crazed murderer.

Hurrying along at his side, Kody tugged at his hand, gasping.

"Wait, just one minute. I just have to breathe!" she said.

And Kody breathed, bending over, bracing her hands on her knees, sweeping in great gulps of air.

Nick looked around anxiously as she did so. Naturally, Dillinger had seen the direction in which they had run.

Nick believed he knew the Everglades better than

Dillinger, at any rate. But, even then, he was praying that Jason Tiger had been watching them, that Tiger had followed him after they had spoken.

"You…you think that Vince will be okay?" Kody asked him.

"He's smart. He needs a good hiding place and he needs to hole up. Dillinger has studied the Everglades on paper, I'm sure. Though he was hoping that the treasure might have been at the mansion, he thought that it might be out here. He had communication going with men who owed him or needed him. I'm sure he has someone coming out here for him soon. But he's not a native. Vince is, right? He seems knowledgeable."

Kody stared at him. "He's knowledgeable. I'm knowledgeable. But this? We're on foot in the swamps! Oh, please! Who is at home out here and knows what they're doing—except for the park rangers and maybe some members of the local tribes and maybe a few members of the Audubon Society. Dillinger was right—we don't know what we're doing out here."

"But Jason Tiger does," Nick reminded her gently.

"Oh! But where is he?"

"He's been watching, I'm sure. He'll find us. Don't worry. Ready?"

She nodded. He grabbed her hand again and hurried in a northwesterly direction, hoping he had followed the directions he'd received from Jason Tiger.

He'd been out in the Everglades often enough. His dad had brought him out here to learn to shoot, and his grandfather had kept a little cabin not far from where they were now. But most of what he knew about the

Everglades he'd learned from a friend, Jimmy Eagle. Jimmy's dad had been a pilot from Virginia but his mom had been Miccosukee.

One of the most important things he'd ever learned from Jimmy was that it was easy to lose track of where you were, easy to think one hammock was another. Waterways changed, and there could be danger in every step for the unsuspecting.

He heard a bird call and stopped walking, returning the call.

A moment later Jason Tiger stepped out onto the path, almost as if he had materialized from the shrubs and trees.

"Right on the mark," he told Nick. "Miss Cameron, excellent."

Kody flushed at the compliment.

"I was excellent at running," she murmured. "But..." She paused, looking at Nick and telling him, "Your expression when you came toward me...it was so...determined."

"I was trying to let you know that we'd be able to do something," Nick told her. "I was going to let you know that Jason had found me while I was looking for the pilings of Anthony Green's distillery operations."

"And Vince chose that moment to run," Kody murmured.

"You think he's alive?" Jason Tiger asked Nick.

"I think it's possible."

"I'll get you to the cabin, then I'll look," Jason said.

"I wanted Kody safe with you," Nick said. "As long as Kody is safe, I can go back out and search until I find Vince—and Floyd. Floyd deserves jail time, but he doesn't deserve a bullet in the back from Dillinger."

"This way," Jason Tiger said.

He led them through a barely discernible trail until they came to the water.

He had a canoe there.

"Hop in," he told them.

Nick steadied the craft and gave Kody a hand. He stepped in carefully himself. Jason hopped in after, shoving his oar into the earth to send them out into the water.

They were in an area of cypress swamps; the trees grew here and there in the water. Egrets, cranes and herons seemed to abound and fish jumped all around them. Nick saw a number of small gators, lazy and seeking the heat of the waning sun.

The sun was going down, he realized. Night was coming again.

Jason drew the canoe toward the shore and then leaped out. Nick did the same, helping to drag the canoe up on the shore.

He wasn't sure what he was expecting, but not the pleasant cabin in the woods he and Kody saw as they burst through the last thick foliage on the trail.

It wasn't any kind of chickee. It was a log cabin, on high ground.

Nick looked at Jason Tiger, who seemed amused.

"There are a lot of houses out here. A lot on tribal lands. We're not completely living in the past, you know. Hey, guys, if it were summer, there's even an air conditioner. Everything here is run on a generator," Jason told them.

"Wow, so, there are a lot of these out here? For the Miccosukee and Seminole?" Kody asked.

Jason laughed. "No. Actually, this one belongs to the United States government. A lot of drug traffic goes through here."

Jason had a key; he used it, letting them into the cabin. It was rustic, offering a sofa in worn leather, a group of chairs, a center stove and a few throw rugs.

"There are bedrooms to the right and left. Hot showers are available—naturally, we ask you to conserve water. I have lots of coffee and power bars and other food."

"You live out here?" Kody asked him.

"When I need to. When we're watching the flow of illegal drugs through the area. I work with a newbie, Sophia Gray, and when she's in residence, she uses the second bedroom. You'll find clean clothing there, Miss Cameron. Anyway, I've been in touch with Special Agent Frasier and the police. We are actually on the edge of National Park land. You're at a safe house. You'll be fine, and we'll have you out of here by morning," Jason told Kody. "And now..."

"I need to get back out there," Nick said. "Find Vince first...and hope that I can find Floyd, as well."

"And Dillinger," Kody said. "He's still out there. He has to be stopped. I think that he really is crazy—dangerously crazy."

"Yes, and Dillinger," Nick said. "And, yes, he is crazy. Functionally crazy, if you will, and that makes him very dangerous." His tone softened as he added directions. "You stay here and obey anything Jason says, and stay safe."

"Of course," Kody said.

"Wait, this is backward. You need to watch over Miss Cameron," Jason said. "I'll see if I can find your friend, Vince, and the others."

"I can't ask you to take on my case," Nick said.

"You have to ask me. I know these hammocks and waterways like the back of my hand. You don't. I'll find them." When Nick was about to protest, he added, "I'm right, and you know that I'm right. I'm better out here than you are, no disrespect intended."

Nick was quiet for a moment and then lowered his head. "All right," he said.

"You're still armed?" Jason asked Nick.

Nick reached for the little holster at his back and the Glock there. "I am armed."

"All right, then. I'm going to head right back out. My superiors at the FBI know this place. We're remote, but they'll get here."

"I should go out with you—"

"But you won't," Jason told him.

Nick nodded. "You're right. You're far better for this job than me."

He felt Kody's fingers slip around his arm. "I'm sorry. You could both go if it weren't for me. Honestly, I know how to lock a door. I can watch out for myself here."

"No way. You're a witness who can put Dillinger away forever," Jason said.

"He's right. We can't risk you."

"Great. Because I'm a witness," Kody murmured.

Jason smiled at them both. "You're okay here for the moment. Take showers, relax. You were both amazing. Miss Cameron, you behaved selflessly, with great courage, and Special Agent Connolly, you're the stuff that makes the Bureau the place to belong. So, take this time. Sit, breathe… Hey, there's real coffee here."

"Thanks, Jason," Nick murmured.

Kody stepped over to Jason and took his hand, shaking it. "Thank you! And the child…the child is really all right?"

"Yes. Thanks to you, they knew where to search. He's safe and sound."

"I'm so glad," Kody murmured.

Jason nodded then and headed to the door. "Lock up," he told Nick. "Not that I'm expecting you'll have any company, but—"

"You just never know," Nick finished for Jason. He offered him a hand, as well. "Thank you, my friend."

"We're all in this together," Jason assured him.

When he left, Nick locked the door.

Kody was heading toward the kitchen. "Coffee!" she said. "Food."

"Yes."

"He's an agent. You're an agent." She spoke while searching the cabinets.

"Yes."

"But you didn't know him before?"

"Yes."

"He's from here and you're from here."

Nick laughed softly. "A lot of people are from here. But, yes—Jason and I went to college together," he said.

"It's ironic, isn't it, that I saw you in New York City? Never here," she said.

He grinned at that. "Millions of people live in this area. I don't suppose it's odd in any way that people from South Florida never met. It's just odd that we wound up here together in this way after we did see each other in New York. I was probably a few years ahead of you in school. I went to Killian—and then on to the University of Florida. I was in Miami-Dade Homicide…and then the FBI," Nick told her. "And, for the last ten months or so, I've been on the task force with Craig. For the last few weeks, I've been undercover as Barrow."

"Incredible," she murmured.

"Not really."

She stared at him a moment longer and then smiled. And he thought that she really was beautiful—a perfect ingénue for whatever play it was she was doing.

She walked over to him.

"Well, I'm alive, thanks to you," she murmured.

"It's my job," he said. "It never should have gone this far. I should have been able to stop Dillinger at the mansion. I should have—"

He suddenly remembered the day she'd brushed by him at Finnegan's. He knew then he would have liked to have met her. Now…

They were safe—relatively safe, at any rate. They'd come far from Dillinger and his insanity. Jason Tiger was a great agent who knew this area and loved it, knew the good, the bad and the ugly of it, and would find and save Vince and Flynn if anyone could.

He would have given so much to smile, think they were back, way back before any of this, imagine that they'd really met, gone out…that he could pull her into his arms, hold her, feel her, kiss her lips…

But Nick was still an agent.

He was still on duty.

"Should have what?" she asked softly.

"Should have been able to finish it all earlier," he said softly.

She still held the bag of coffee. He took it gently from her fingers and headed into the kitchen to measure it out. In no time, he heard the sound as it began to perc.

She still stood in the living room of the cabin, looking out. He saw that she walked to the door to assure herself it was locked. She turned, probably aware that he was studying her.

"Windows?" she asked with a grimace. "I'm usually not the paranoid type."

"They've got locks, I'm sure," Nick said. He crossed the room to join her at the left window to check.

It was impossible.

They'd been crawling around in fetid swamp water, muck and more. Yet there was still something sweet and alluring in her scent.

She looked at him. Her face was close, so close. Her lips…so tempting.

Get a grip! he told himself.

"We should check them all," she said.

"That's a plan. Then all we need fear is a raccoon coming down the chimney," he said, grinning at her.

They checked and double-checked one another, close and closer. He headed to each of the two bedrooms. Simple, rustic, charming, clean…

Equipped with beds.

"This is good, right?" Kody asked him, tugging at the left bedroom window. It was evidently Jason Tiger's room. It was neat as a pin, but there were toiletries on the dresser and some folded clothes on the footrest.

"Yeah." Nick double-checked the window. "One more room," he said.

In the second room, the guest room, he could almost smell the scent of crisp, cool, cotton sheets.

Kody checked a window; he walked over to her.

How the hell could her hair still smell like some kind of subtle, sweet shampoo?

"Good, right?" she asked.

He inhaled the scent. "Yep, excellent."

"And you're still armed?" she asked.

"I am. Glock in the holster at the back of my belt."

"Then it's good. It's really all good. We aren't in any danger."

Nick arched a brow.

They weren't in any danger?

He was pretty sure he was in the worst danger he'd been in since he'd started on his undercover odyssey.

Because she was danger.

Because he was falling into love/lust/respect/admiration…

And he was an agent.

And she was the bartending actress he was duty-bound to protect.

And yet the mind could be a cruel beast at times. No matter what the circumstances, no matter what their danger, his position, her position, he couldn't help but believe there was a future. And in that future they were together.

Or was that just his mind teasing him?

For the moment he needed to shape up and damn the taunting beast of a voice within him that made him picture her as she headed for the shower.

Chapter Eight

Clean!

There was nothing like the feeling of being clean.

Kody could have stayed in the shower forever, except, of course, she knew the water was being heated by a generator. Special Agent Nick Connolly certainly deserved his share of the water.

And Vince was still out there, somewhere. Was he safe? He surely knew more about the Everglades than Dillinger, but just living in the area and knowing history and geography did not ensure survival. There were just too many pitfalls. Crocodilians, snakes, insects—and, of course, a madman running around with a gun.

And what about Floyd?

Floyd was a criminal but not a killer; he had never wanted to hurt them.

She couldn't help but be worried about them both.

She had to believe that Jason Tiger would find Vince. Meanwhile, Vince was smart enough to watch out for sinkholes, gator holes and quicksand. He knew which snakes were harmful and which were not. He probably even had a sense of direction. He would head straight for the observation tower at Shark Valley—and the Tamiami Trail. He was going to be okay.

Hair washed, flesh scrubbed, Kody emerged from the shower. A towel had been easy to find in the bathroom. She hesitated when she was dry, feeling as if she was somewhat of an invader as she headed to the dresser and found clothing that belonged to Jason Tiger's "newbie" associate. "Forgive me," she murmured aloud, finding panties and a bra and then a pair of jeans and a tailored cotton shirt.

When she returned to the living room, Nick was sipping coffee at the little dining table that sat between the kitchen and the living room. He'd obviously showered; his hair was wet and slicked back. She couldn't help but notice the definition of his muscles in a borrowed polo shirt and jeans. She met his eyes, so beyond blue, and she felt such a tug of attraction that she needed to remind herself they were still in a perilous position.

And that Nick had been her captor—who had turned into her savior.

There was surely a name for the confusion plaguing her!

"Hey," he said softly.

"Hey."

"Feel better?"

"I feel terrific," she told him. "Clean. Strong. Okay—still worried."

"Jason will find Vince," he assured her.

She nodded and pulled out a chair to join him at the table. "What are you doing?" she asked him.

He swept an arm out, indicating the maps on the

table. "I'm following your lead. This map was created by a park ranger about ten years ago. Now, of course, mangrove islands pop up here and there, water washes away what was almost solid. You have your hardwood hammocks and you have areas where the hardwood hammocks almost collide with the limestone shelves. From what I'm seeing here and where we've been, I'm convinced that we were in the right place. Anthony Green's still sat on a limestone shelf."

"Where we were today, I'm pretty sure," Kody agreed.

"Exactly. Well, on this map, the ranger—Howard Reece—also made note of the manmade structures he found, or the remnants thereof. Kody, you were right, I believe." He paused and pointed out notations on the map. "There are the pilings for different chickee huts he had going there. Back quarter—that's the one where Anthony Green did his bookkeeping. So, if you're right, that's where we'll find the buried treasure."

"If it does exist," she said.

"I believe that it does."

"And you want to go find it—now?"

He laughed softly. "Nope. I want to stay right here now. Stay right here until you're picked up by my people and taken to safety. Then I want to help Jason Tiger and the forces we'll get out here to find Vince and Floyd. And then, at some point, get the right people with the right equipment out here to see if we're right or wrong."

She nodded and bit into her lower lip.

He reached out, laying his hand over hers where it

rested on the table. "I know that you're worried. It will be okay. Jason will find Vince, and, I hope, Floyd."

"What if he can't find them? What if he can't find either of them?" Kody asked.

"He will." The conviction with which he spoke the words sank into her, giving her hope. "For now," he said, "let's find something to eat. There's not a lot of food here, nothing fresh, but there are a lot of cans and, as Jason said, power bars."

"There's soup," Kody said, pointing to a shelf in the kitchen area.

"Anything sounds good. Want me to cook for you?"

"You mean open a can?"

"Exactly."

Kody laughed. "Yes, I'd love you to open a can for me."

The both rose. Nick dug around for a can-opener. Kody found bowls, spoons and even napkins. She set the table.

"Nice," Nick told her.

"Well, we want to be civilized, right?"

"I don't know. I could suck the stone-cold food out of a can right now, but, hey, you're right. Heated is going to be better."

She smiled. It was an oddly domestic scene as they put their meal of soup and crackers together. Jason kept a hefty supply of bottled water at the cabin, and the water tasted delicious.

"So, when you're not playing the part of a thug and holding up historic properties, what are you doing?" Kody asked as she ate.

"I'm with the same unit as Craig Frasier—criminal investigation," Nick told her. "New York City is my home office. The man you know as Dillinger was carrying out a number of criminal activities in New York that included extortion and murder. He served time. He should have served more time, after. The cops had arrested him again a few years ago on an armed robbery, but the one witness was found floating in the East River. Then he started to move south, so we followed his activities. And as I said, I was a natural to slide into the gang he was forming down here."

"And you like your work?" Kody asked. "I know that Craig likes his work and his office."

"I love what I do. It feels right," he said. "What about you—what do you do when you're not guarding the booth? Ah, yes! Acting. And you're friends with Kevin Finnegan." He was quiet for a minute. "Well, this is just rude, but what kind of friends?"

She laughed. "Real friends. We've struggled together on a number of occasions. We met on the set of a long-running cop show that we both had a few short roles on." She grinned. "He was the victim and I was the killer once in the same episode. And we've gone to some of the same workshops together. But, trust me, we were never anything but friends."

"Kevin is a good-looking, great guy," Nick said.

"That he is," she agreed. "And it's cool to have a friend like him for auditioning and heading out and trying to see what's going on. We were both accepted to a really prestigious class once because we could call on one another right away and work together. We decided long ago that we'd never ruin what we had by dating or becoming friends with benefits, or anything like that." She hesitated, flushing. That was way too much information, she told herself. "And, by the way, Kevin is in love. It's even a secret from me, it's such a hush-hush thing. I hope it works out for him. I do love him—as a friend."

"Nice," he murmured.

He was watching her, his eyes so intense she looked away uncomfortably.

She rose uneasily, afraid it sounded as if she was determined he know she wasn't involved with Kevin. She wandered closer to the stove and nervously poured more coffee into her cup. "So. What happens now? I mean, Jason Tiger has been in contact with Craig and the FBI and the local police, right? They'll be out soon, right?"

"They'll be out soon," he agreed. "We're just in an area where there is no easy access. But they'll get here. Why don't you try to get some sleep? You have to be exhausted."

"I'm fine, really. Well, I'm not fine. I'm worried about Vince. I just wish—"

"Jason Tiger is good. For all we know, he might have found Vince by now."

"Right," she murmured. She smiled at him. "I can't believe that I didn't know you right away. I mean, it's not as if we got to know one another that night at Finnegan's. But you do have a really unusual eye color and…"

"I was afraid that you'd recognize me," he said quietly. "That, naturally, you would call me out, and we would all be dead."

"Yes, well…"

"I just wasn't that memorable," he said, a slight smile teasing his lips.

"Oh, no! I had been thinking…"

"Yes?"

Kody flushed, shaking her head.

"You know what I was thinking?" he asked.

"What's that?"

"I was thinking that it was a damned shame that I was on this assignment, that I never had asked you out, that I was meeting you as an armed and masked criminal."

"Oh," she said softly.

He stood and joined her by the stove. Stopping close to her, he touched her chin, lifting it slightly.

"What if it had been different? What if we'd met again in New York and I'd asked you to a show…to dinner? Would you have said yes?"

Kody was afraid her knees would give way. She was usually so confident. Okay, so maybe being under siege, kidnapped at gunpoint and still trapped in a swamp was making her a little too emotional. She was still shaky. Still caught by those eyes. And she was attracted to him as she couldn't remember being attracted to anyone before.

"Yes," she said softly.

He smiled, his fingers still gentle on her chin. He moved toward her and she could almost taste his kiss, imagine the hunger, the sweetness.

Then there was a pounding on the door.

Dropping his hands from her chin, he moved quickly away from her, heading to the door.

"It's Tiger!" came a call.

Nick opened the bolt on the door. Jason Tiger was there with Vince. Vince was shaking.

And bleeding.

"Oh, get in, get in! Sit him down. I'll boil water. Is an ambulance coming? Can an ambulance come?" Kody demanded.

Nick took Vince's weight, leading him to a chair. Apparently both men were adept at dealing with wounds. Nick had Vince's shirt ripped, while Jason went for his first-aid box.

Kody did set water to boil.

"It's just a flesh wound," Nick said.

"We'll get it cleaned, get some antiseptic on it," Jason murmured.

Nick took the clean, hot towel Kody provided and in moments they discovered he had been right; it was just a flesh wound.

"Dillinger didn't shoot you?" Kody asked.

Vince looked up at her with a shrug. "I tripped on a root. Scratched myself on a branch."

"Oh," she said, relieved, sliding down to sit in one of the chairs.

"Floyd?" Nick asked Jason Tiger.

"No sign of him—nor have I been able to find Dillinger. The airboat is where it was. He hasn't taken off from where you were, by the old distillery."

Vince suddenly turned and grabbed Nick's arm. "You weren't one of them. You're not a crook."

"No," Nick said, hunkering down and easing himself from Vince's hold. There wasn't time to give him the background of his undercover investigation right now. They had to find Dillinger. "You were smart—and lucky. When Dillinger started shooting, you went down low. But he is still out there. As long as he's out there, other people are in danger. Did you see him again? Did you hear him stalking you?"

Vince looked from Nick to Jason and then at Nick again. "I think he chased me through half of the hammock. Then he was gone."

"I didn't see him," Jason said.

Nick stood. "All right." He looked over at Jason Tiger. "This time, I think it's me. I think that I need to go," he said.

Tiger nodded.

"You're going out there again?" Kody asked him.

"Yes, we need to stop Dillinger and, hopefully, find Floyd alive."

He turned, heading out of the little cabin in the swamp. Even as he did so, they heard shouts. Kody hurried to the door behind Jason.

An airboat had arrived; it bore a number of men in khaki uniforms.

Men with guns.

They were going after the killer in the swamps.

"Kody!"

One of the men, she saw, was hurrying toward her. It was Craig Frasier. He caught her up in a hug.

"Thank God. Kieran and Kevin have been going insane, they've been so worried about you. Not to mention your family. We'll get you home. We'll get you back to safety."

She gave him a hug back. Craig was truly an amazing man. Kody was happy that he and Kieran Finnegan were together—and happy that he was a good friend to Kevin and all of the Finnegan family.

She was grateful to know him, and everyone involved with Finnegan's on Broadway.

He was there for her.

She and Vince were safe.

And yet, at that moment—right when she was surrounded by law enforcement—she felt bereft.

Nick was gone. He was off with the teams of officers that had come out to find Dillinger and Floyd.

EMTs had arrived with the officers; they were looking at Vince's wounds. They were asking her if she was all right.

Soon, she was escorted onto an airboat. And before she knew it, she was back on the Tamiami Trail, headed toward downtown Miami and to the home in the Roads section of the city, just north of Coconut Grove, where she had grown up. A policewoman came with her, took her statement and promised to watch her house through the night—just in case Dillinger found his way to her before they were able to find Dillinger.

And there was nothing left to do except watch the television to see how the rest of it all began to unfold.

DILLINGER WAS OUT THERE. He was determined to get the treasure, and so, Nick was certain, he had to have stayed in the general area where they had been.

Law enforcement had fanned out, but by the time they reached the hammock again, the airboat that Dillinger had extorted from the men he had been blackmailing was gone. He was off, somewhere.

The forces that had come out for the search were from Miami-Dade and Monroe counties, Florida Highway Patrol, the U.S. Marshal's Office and the FBI.

But, as the hours went by, they found nothing.

Nick was about to give it up himself when he determined one more time to search the original hammock. The grasses grew high there, and a twisted pattern of pines might hide just about anything along the northern edge of the hammock.

He came out alone and stood in the center, as still as he could manage. And that was when he was certain he heard movement. He cautiously took a step, and then another, and drew his weapon and gave out a warning. "FBI. Show yourself, hands above your head."

Floyd emerged out of the grass. He was shaking visibly.

"I don't want to die. I don't want to die. They can lock me up, but I don't want to die."

"You're not going to die. But you are under arrest."

"Barrow. You," Floyd said. "I should have known you were a cop. I mean, I don't like blood and guts. But you…? Wow. I should have guessed it. It's cool. It doesn't matter. Get me in. Protect me. He was running around here crazy. Dillinger, I mean. He wants me dead. He wants you dead more but…" He shook his head as he stepped forward. "Get me out of here. Quickly. He'll shoot me dead right here in front of all of you, he just wants me dead so badly."

"All right, all right," Nick said, and cuffed the man. He caught him by the elbow and hurried back toward the airboat where other officers were waiting. "Come on, we'll get you in. You'll be safe."

"Did you get him? Did you get Dillinger?" Floyd asked.

"Not yet."

"You have to get him."

"Yes, we know."

But while Floyd was brought in, and they worked through the night, there was no sign of Dillinger to be found.

When morning dawned, he was still on the loose.

KODY SIPPED COFFEE and watched the news.

She should have slept, but she hadn't.

Her parents had arrived as soon as humanly possible, of course. They'd been worried sick about her, and she understood.

They'd nearly crushed her. Her mother had cried. Her father had cursed the day he'd discovered he'd been related to the Crystal family. Emotions had soared and then, thankfully, fallen back to earth and she had finally managed to make her parents behave normally once again.

She'd gotten a call from Mayor Holden Burke. He'd nearly been in tears as they had spoken. He'd been told by the police that it had been her courage against the kidnappers that had led to his son being found. She'd told him how grateful she was that the boy, Adrian, was alive, and she'd begged him not to do anything publicly for her—she wanted it all to remain low key.

"Yes, but I hear you're an actress—don't you want the publicity?" he'd asked.

She'd laughed. "No, I want to create characters and read well for auditions and, of course, get great reviews," she told him. "The only publicity I want is for great performances. As far as my home goes… I just worry."

"Oh, trust me," he assured her, "more people than ever will want to tour the house now. And I will thank you with my whole heart and remain low key."

When she hung up, she'd smiled, glad of a new friend.

She needed to sleep.

But hours later she was back up, staring at the television. She wanted to hear about Nick.

Every local channel and even the national channels had covered the news.

Nathan Appleby, aka Dillinger, was still on the loose. The FBI had been on his trail for nearly a year, from the northeast down to the far south. Thanks, however, to the combined efforts of various law-enforcement groups, the hostages taken at the Crystal Manor were safe, as were those who had been forced to accompany the criminals. Three of the gang had been killed; their bodies had been recovered by the Coast Guard and the Miccosukee police.

Dillinger, however, was still at large. The local populace was advised that he was armed and extremely dangerous.

There was nothing said about Nick Connolly.

"Hey!"

She had been sitting in the living room, quietly watching the television. She turned to see that her father was already up, as well.

She smiled and patted the sofa next to her. He came and sat with her.

"The manhunt continues?" he asked.

"Here's the thing. Dillinger manipulates people. The men who brought him the airboat—they weren't bad. I mean, I don't think they would ever want to hurt anyone. Dillinger put them into a desperate situation, like he does with everyone."

With an arm around her shoulders, her father said, "I didn't want you moving to New York. And I didn't want to stop you. You have to follow your dreams, and you're responsible and…well, now I'm glad you're going to be in New York—far, far away from wherever the Anthony Green stash might be. I thank God that you were rescued. I can't imagine what your mom and I would have gone through if we had made it home and…and you hadn't been found."

"I'm very thankful."

"You don't ever have to work at that awful mansion again—under any circumstances!"

"Dad, the house wasn't at fault. I love the old house and the history—and we don't throw it all away because of a very bad man. They will find him."

He nodded. “I know. For your mom and me, you’re everything, though. We thought it was tough when you decided to move to New York, when you landed the role and you got the part-time gig at Finnegan’s. But… you were safer there.”

“None of us can ever expect something like what happened, Dad. Anywhere. Bad people exist everywhere.”

“I know,” he told her quietly. “Because of New York, though, you already knew that FBI man who brought you home.”

“Craig Frasier. Yes, I know him through Kieran Finnegan, who is Kevin’s sister. You met Kevin—I introduced you to him when we were in an infomercial together.”

“Right.”

“His family owns the pub where I’ll be working part-time. And you will love it when you come up,” Kody assured her father.

“And he’s the one who saved you?”

Kody shook her head. “No. That was Nick.”

“They haven’t even mentioned a Nick on the news, you know.”

“I know. He was working undercover. But… ” Her voice trailed.

“Well, if he weren’t all right and still working this thing, you’d be hearing about a dead agent,” her father said.

“Dad!”

“Am I right?”

“Yes, you’re right.”

She leaned against his shoulder. “Don’t blame the house on Crystal Island, Dad. Don’t stop loving it. Don’t stop caring about it. If we do that, we let the bad guys win, you know.”

“Very nobly said,” her father told her, a slight smile twisting his lips. “But…I say screw all noble thoughts when it comes to your safety!”

“Dad!”

“Not really. I just want them to catch that guy!”

Kody agreed.

And she longed to hear that Nick Connolly was fine, as well.

TWO DAYS LATER there were still a number of officers searching through the miles and miles that encompassed the enormous geographical body known as the Everglades.

Nick was no longer among them.

The chase now would fall to the men who knew the area.

He spent a day being debriefed and a day on paperwork. That was part of it, too.

He was going to be given a commendation. Thanks to his work, according to Director Egan via a video conference, a kidnapped child had been found and not a hostage had been harmed.

In his debriefing, Nick was determined that the agency understand it had been Dakota Cameron who had gotten the information out of Nathan Appleby and that Jason Tiger had been the one to convey it to the police and the FBI back in Miami. He was told that

Kody had completely downplayed her role in the entire event, hoping that life could get back to normal.

He, too, would stay out of the public eye. It didn't pay, in his position, to have his face plastered on newspapers across the country.

Floyd—aka Gary Forman—had told the police everything he knew about Dillinger, the gang and the various enterprises that Dillinger had been into. What seemed surprising to Nick at the end of it all was that Dillinger was an amazing crook. The man had worked with a scope that Nick, even as part of the gang, had merely been able to guess about.

Sitting with Craig Frasier in the Miami Bureau offices, he shook his head and said, "Why did the man become so obsessed with a treasure that may not exist? If he stayed away from Crystal Island, he could still be fronting all his illicit operations."

"Who says he isn't? The man is still out there," Craig reminded him.

"So he is. But he's known. His face is known. The thing is, of course, that he does use people."

"Exactly. He may well be deep in Mexico now, on an island somewhere—or headed for the Rockies. No one knows with a man like that."

"True," Nick said. "There was just something about him and that treasure. He was obsessed, like an addict. He still means to get that treasure somehow."

"Well, Jason Tiger and the local Miccosukee police as well as the FBI and city and county police are still on it."

"Yes," Nick murmured. "Good people. And still…I don't feel right. I don't feel that we should be turning it over now. You and me—we followed Nathan Appleby all the way down the east coast. I was the one chosen to go undercover."

"Something that is completely blown now, of course—albeit in the best way."

"Yes. It doesn't feel right, though."

"And we're due on a plane back to New York tomorrow. It's over for us. I thought you'd be glad. I know that you didn't mind and accepted the undercover—but, it's also damned good to get out of it."

"I am ready, I don't mind doing what's needed, but you're right—there's a time you're ready for out. There's always the point where you may have to give yourself away or commit a criminal act. And then you have guys like Nathan Appleby—guys who kidnap kids and don't give a damn if they live or die, as long as the act gives them their leverage. I am glad it's over. I just wanted it to be over with Nathan Appleby behind bars."

"We don't win every time. We try our best. That's what we do."

Nick stood and grinned at Craig. "Tomorrow, hmm. What time?"

"Plane leaves at 11:00 a.m."

"I'll be there."

"And tonight?"

"Tonight…I want to stop by and see a girl. I want to pretend that months and months haven't gone by and that I just saw her say hi to you and smile at me as she left a restaurant."

"And?"

Nick laughed softly. "And, hopefully, I'm going on a date."

Chapter Nine

An iconic pop singer died. An earthquake rattled Central America. A boatload of refugees made landfall just south of Homestead, and a rising politician threw his hat into the ring for a vacated senate seat.

Given all that, the news about the assault on the historic mansion on Crystal Island at last died down.

Kody had spent hours with her folks, assuring them she was fine. She had made arrangements for them to fly to New York when the show opened, and she'd told them about her apartment, her part-time job and her friends, especially the Finnegans. She told them about the four siblings who owned the pub. How Declan was the boss and Kieran was a clinical psychologist and therapist who often worked with the police and the FBI. How Danny was a super tour guide and would take them around and, as they knew, Kevin was an actor.

It was all good.

She went back out to the mansion. She and her co-workers and friends who had been taken hostage hugged and cried and did all the things that survivors did. She was somewhat surprised to discover that none of them was leaving.

"I just don't see it happening again," Vince said.

"You don't give in to violence," Stacey Carlson told her.

Nan Masters, his supportive assistant, as always, smiled. "Stacey does not give in. He hires more security. That's the way we roll."

Jose was still in the hospital, but doing well.

Brandi was fine, as well—traumatized, but fine.

Kody felt relieved and almost happy when she left them. Everything was perfect.

She'd called Craig; he'd assured her that Nick Connolly was fine. They were all disappointed, of course, that they hadn't been able to find Nathan Appleby.

Her parents were still at a board meeting, seeing to the trust, when Kody came back from the mansion and turned on the news.

Yes. The story had already fallen to the back burner.

The doorbell rang as she was staring at the television.

When she looked through the peephole, her heart skipped a beat. It was Nick.

She instantly thrust the door open.

"Hey! You're supposed to be cautious!" he began.

He was barely able to speak. She threw her arms around him, holding him fiercely.

"Um, cautious…or not!" he said, looking down into her eyes, half detangling himself and half sweeping her closer. And he just looked at her and then his mouth touched down on hers and he kissed her.

Her mouth parted and she tasted the sweet heat of his lips and tongue. The warmth swept into her limbs, magical and wonderful, and causing her to tremble. He lifted his mouth from hers, searching out her eyes.

"You're okay," she said as if she needed him to confirm it.

"Yes. And you?"

"Absolutely fine, thank you. I… You're here. Thank you. I mean, thank you for knowing that I would be worried about you. And thank you for letting me know that you're okay."

"That's not why I'm here," he said. "Although I'm grateful to know that you were worried."

"Of course," she murmured. "So, why are you here?"

"Ah, yes. Well, you're not being held by a demonic kidnapper anymore. I'm not working undercover. In fact, I'm free until tomorrow, when I fly back to New York. I'm here to ask you to dinner. This is your family home, though, I understand. Should I ask your folks, too?"

"No! Oh, don't get me wrong. I love them dearly. But I don't need their approval to tell you this. I would love to go to dinner with you. That would be great. Where should we go?"

"I'm staying at the Legend, the new place on the bay. They have a chef who just won the grand prize on a reality show," he said with a rueful smile. "Want to try it?"

"Yes. Give me one minute." She started into the house, leaving him on the steps, then went back to invite him in. Gathering her wits, she ran to the kitchen counter to leave a note for her parents so they wouldn't worry, grabbed her purse and headed back. He smiled, watching her.

"What?" she asked.

"I was nervous coming here to ask you out, and I can see you're nervous, too. But we shouldn't be so nervous. We know each other, right? We slept together—kind of—in a hut."

"Yes…but it's different now, huh?"

He offered her his arm. She took it and then headed down the walk to his rental car, a black Subaru. He opened the door for her; she slid in.

"They still haven't found Dillinger—Nathan Appleby?" she asked.

"No. It's amazing that he's managed to disappear the way he has—and yet, not. He has such a network going. He had a way to reach someone who got him out—or got him into hiding in the Everglades, one or the other."

"But you're going home, right?"

"Yes. I wouldn't be useful anymore undercover. He knows me. Craig Frasier is heading back, too. The operation will be handled from here now. Every agency down here is on the lookout."

"You don't sound happy about it," Kody said.

"I'm not. I hate it when we haven't finished what we started out to do. Dillinger has been a step ahead of us down the eastern seaboard. I'm not happy, but…" He shrugged, glancing over at her. "But you're heading to New York City, too, right?"

"The play opens in a few weeks."

"Living theater?" he asked. "I mean, isn't most theater living? Not to sound too ignorant or anything, but..."

Kody laughed. "Interactive would be a better description. It's been done before in a similar manner. We're doing a Shakespeare play, except that it all takes place on different floors within an old hotel. I love what we're doing. It's never the same thing, different every night. Basically, we are the characters. We work with the script and draw people in from the audience. And the audience moves from place to place while we have our scenes in which we work."

"I can't wait to see it."

"You'd really come?"

"Sure. We can have FBI night at the theater."

"Very amusing."

"I'm serious. I'm sure that Craig and Kieran will come, and Craig's partner. And once I'm home, I'm hoping to be paired again with my old partner, Sherri Haskell."

"Ah, Sherri."

"Married to Mo."

"I didn't ask."

"Yes, you did."

Nick drew up to valet parking and they left the car behind.

He caught Kody's hand, hurrying up the planked ramp that led out to the bay and along the water. The moon was a crescent, dozens of stars were shining and the glow of lights from the hotel and restaurant on the water was magical.

"Florida will always be home," Nick said.

"Always," Kody agreed. He pulled her into his arms and he kissed her again, and she thought that, indeed, it was all magic. She couldn't remember when she had met someone who made her feel this way, when she had longed for just such a touch and just such a kiss.

He drew away from her and leaned against the rail, just holding her, smoothing her hair, looking out on the water.

"You have a room?" she asked softly.

"That's a leading question, you know."

"Yes, I know."

He studied her eyes. "Room service?"

"That would be lovely."

He caught her hand again and led her to the elevator. When he opened the door to his room, she went straight to the large window that looked out on the night.

"Sorry, there's no balcony. Not on taxpayers' money," he said. "However, it is much better than the place I had before, when I was hanging with Dillinger's gang."

She turned to look at him.

"It wouldn't matter to me where you stayed," she said.

He strode to her, taking her into his arms. She drew the backs of her fingers down his face. He kissed her again, his fingers sliding to the zipper at the back of her dress. She allowed it to slip from her body.

"I wasn't… I'm not really prepared," he told her. Then he laughed. "I'm sure I can be—there're a dozen stores nearby."

"I'm on the pill," she told him.

"I'm not— There's no one else at the moment?" he asked.

She shook her head. "I've been working on the play, on the move…on life. But I've always been an optimist."

He laughed at that, pulled her closer. And he slid from his jacket, doffed his holster and gun, and kissed her neck and throat while she struggled with the buttons on his shirt. Still half dressed, they fell back on the bed. He kissed her again and then again, and stared down at her, and she reached up to him, drawing him back and tugging at his belt and his waistband.

Rolling, mingling passionate kisses with laughter, they finally stripped one another completely and lay breathlessly naked together, frozen for a moment of sweet anticipation and wonder. Then they tangled together again, seeking to press their lips upon one another's flesh here and there. He rose above her, staring down at her, straddled over her, and she reached for him, amazed that however it had come about, they were here together, and she was simply grateful.

He kissed her lips, her throat, and his mouth moved along her body, teasing her flesh. She lay still for a moment, not even breathing, swept up by the sensation. He caressed and teased, lower and lower, until she could stay still no longer, and she arched and writhed and rolled with him, and allowed her lips and tongue to tease in turn, bathing the length of him in kisses until breathless, they came together at last. He moved within her slowly at first. Their eyes were locked as the pace of their lovemaking began to increase, bit by bit, to a fever pitch.

Outside, the stars shone on the water. A breeze drifted by. The night was beautiful and, for Kody, these were intricate and unbelievable moments in which the world was nothing but stars, the scent of shimmering seawater and the man who held her.

Their climax was volatile and incredible, and holding one another in sweet aftershocks seemed just as wonderful. And then whispering and laughing and talking—and wondering if they should indeed order room service or just let the concept of dinner go—seemed as natural as if they had known one another forever.

"So there's been no one in your life for a long time?" he asked her.

"Not in a long time. I do love what I do. Rehearsals are long and hard—then there is the part-time work, as you know. And you?"

"Long hours, too. But I was engaged. To a designer."

"A designer?"

"Marissa works for a major clothing line. She wants her own one day."

"What happened?"

"Off hours, not enough time…we drifted apart. I have nothing bad to say about her. We just—we just weren't meant to be. Being with an agent isn't easy.

Takes someone who understands that time is precious and elusive."

"It's a give and take," Kody said softly. She hoisted up on an elbow and smiled down at him. "I had a similar problem with my last ex. Gerard."

"Ah. And what happened to him?"

Kody hesitated. "He met a teacher. She didn't work a second job to pay for the privilege of doing her main job. She just had much better hours."

"I'm sorry."

"I introduced him to the teacher," Kody said. "He was a good guy. I wasn't right for him."

"You think we might be right for each other?" Nick asked softly.

"I just… I hope," Kody said.

"Hmm. What made you…care about me?"

"Your ethics."

"As a crook?"

She laughed. "You wouldn't hurt people. That mattered. And you?"

"Well, there's nothing wrong with the way you look, you know," he teased.

"Ah. So it's all physical attraction, then?"

"And your courage, determination and attitude," he said.

She laughed softly. "For me it was your eyes. I knew your eyes. And I knew you, because of your eyes."

He smiled and pulled her down to him again. And what started as a kiss developed into another session of lovemaking.

By the time they finished, Kody jumped up after

looking at her watch. "Oh! I have to go back. My parents… I mean, I was just home here to tie up loose ends. My mother and father are already a bit crazy."

"Say no more. I'll get you home right away," Nick promised.

They dressed quickly. "I really did intend to wine and dine you with a sumptuous meal," Nick said, his hand at the small of her back as they left the room and headed down.

"We'll both be in New York. There are tons of fabulous restaurants there, too, you know. I mean, I am assuming that we'll see one another in New York? Or is that maybe too much of an assumption? I was really worried about myself, you know. I was attracted to you—when you were with Dillinger. You weren't a killer—I knew that much…well, my feelings did make me question myself."

He smiled, holding her hand tight.

"Time is precious and elusive," he said. "I will gratefully accept any you can give me in the city—especially with your show starting."

"I'll find time," she promised. "I'm partial to old, historic restaurants."

"I know a great pub. I think we both get a discount there, too," Nick teased.

"A great pub!" she agreed.

The valet brought Nick's car. Kody glanced at her watch again. It was nearly 1:00 a.m. She was surprised that her mother or her father hadn't called her yet. Maybe they were happy she was out with an FBI agent.

The distance between the hotel and her parents' home wasn't great; she was there within minutes.

Nick walked her to the door.

"I'll really see you in New York?" she murmured.

He pulled her into his arms. "You will see me. You'll see so much of me..."

She moved into his kiss. The wonder of the night seemed to settle over her like a cloak. She was tempted to walk into her house and check on her family—and then just tell them she was off to sleep with her FBI agent before he had to get on his plane.

Kody managed to gather a sense of decorum.

"I should meet your parents," Nick said. "But I guess you shouldn't wake them up."

"Probably not the best idea," she agreed. "You'll meet them. They're coming up for opening night."

They kissed again. It seemed all but impossible to stop—to let him drive away.

But, finally, he broke away. "Kody, I..."

"Me, too," she said softly.

Then she slipped into the house, closed the door behind her and leaned against it. A sense of euphoria seemed to have settled over her.

She was walking on air.

But as she moved away from the front door, the lamp above her father's living room chair went on.

"Dad," she murmured.

Then she fell silent.

And she dead-stopped.

It wasn't her father, sitting in his chair.

It was Nathan Appleby—aka Dillinger.

NICK HEADED DOWN to the rental Subaru but paused as he reached the car. He looked up at the sky. It really was one of the most fantastic winter nights in Miami. Stars brilliant against the black velvet of the sky, a moon that seemed almost to smile in a half curve and a balmy temperature of maybe seventy degrees.

He would always love South Florida as home. There was nothing like it—even when it came to the Everglades with all its glory, from birds of uncanny beauty, endangered panthers—and deadly reptiles.

It would always be home to both of them, even as it seemed they both loved New York City and embraced all that could be found there. Actually, Nick had never cared much which office he was assigned to; he was just glad to be with the Bureau. Even if they didn't win every time.

Nathan Appleby was still out there.

But the hostages were safe. The hostages were alive. It was out of his hands and, after tonight, he could say that it had ended exceptionally well. The future loomed before them.

He turned the key in the ignition and drove out onto the street. His phone rang and he glanced at the Caller ID. It was Kody. He answered it quickly. "Hello?"

At first there was nothing. He almost hung up, thinking maybe she had pocket dialed him.

Then he heard Kody's voice. "You know me, Mr. Appleby. You know that I won't help you unless I'm sure others are safe. And this time, you have my parents. Do you really think that I'll do anything for you, anything at all, when I'm worried about their safety?"

"Right now, Miss Cameron, they are alive. You know me. I don't care a lot whether people live or die. You get that treasure for me and your parents live. It's that simple."

Nick quickly pulled the car to the side. He hadn't gone more than a block from the Cameron house. He cursed himself a thousand times over.

They had underestimated Nathan Appleby. They hadn't comprehended the depth of his obsession, realized that he would risk everything to find the Anthony Green treasure.

Appleby had known everything about the Crystal Island mansion, about Anthony Green. It was only natural that he should have known where the Cameron family lived, only natural that he had made his way out of the Everglades and into the city of Miami—and on to the Cameron house.

"You left Adrian Burke bound and gagged in an abandoned crack house," Nick heard Kody say. "I need to know where my parents are—that they will be safe. That's the only way I help you."

"Okay, here it is. They are not in a crack house. They're out on a boat belonging to some very good friends of mine. Now, you help me and I get the treasure, I make a call and they go free. If you don't come with me—nicely!—I call and they take an eternal swim in Biscayne Bay. Oh, and added insurance—if they don't hear from me every hour, your parents take a dive."

"I'll go with you. But what guarantee do I have?"

"You don't have any guarantees. No guarantees at

all. But…I can dial right now. Mommy and Daddy do love the water, right?"

"Do you mind if I put sneakers on?" Kody asked. "They beat the hell out of sandals for scrounging around in the Everglades!"

TORTURE WAS ILLEGAL.

But Nick still considered slipping into the Cameron house and slicing Nathan Appleby to ribbons in order to force him to tell the truth about Kody's parents.

But there were inherent dangers—such as Appleby getting a message through to the people holding Kody's parents, Kody herself protesting, and a million other things that could go wrong—along with torture being illegal. Appleby had said he had to make a call once an hour. The man was mean enough, manic enough, to die before making a call.

Nick didn't want to give up the phone; he couldn't reach Craig or anyone else unless he did hang up the phone.

He knew where Appleby would take Kody.

"Let's go!" he heard Appleby snap. "Ditch the purse—you have a phone in there, right? Ditch the purse now!"

The line was still open but nothing else was coming from it. Nick hung up quickly and called Craig.

"We'll get the Coast Guard out in the bay along with local police," Craig said as soon as Nick apprised him of the situation. "We'll find them. Swing by for me at the hotel. We'll head out together. They'll alert Jason

Tiger and he'll see that everyone out there is watching and ready."

"We know where they're going," Nick said.

"How damned crazy can that man be? He intends to dig in the swamp all night by himself?"

"He's not alone. He has Kody."

NATHAN APPLEBY MADE Kody drive.

Her own car.

She wasn't sure why that seemed to add insult to injury.

She didn't know how he'd gotten to her house; she hadn't seen a car, but then, he might have parked anywhere on the street.

Wherever he had come from, he had come to her house and kidnapped her parents. They were out somewhere in the bay. He'd come prepared; he had two backpacks—one she was certain she was supposed to be carrying through the Everglades. He'd managed all this with the news displaying his picture constantly and every law-enforcement agent in the city on the lookout for him.

He kept his gun trained on her as they drove, held low in the seat lest someone note that she was driving under stress.

Not that there were that many people out. Miami was truly a city that never slept, but here, in the residential areas that led from her home close to downtown and west toward the Everglades, there were few cars on the road.

"I'm not sure how you think I'm doing this. I mean,

honestly? I don't know how I'm doing this. I've only ever dropped by the Everglades by daylight. I'm pretty sure there are gates or fences or something when you get to the park entrances," Kody said.

"We won't be taking a park entrance," he told her.

"What? You just happen to have friends with access driveways?" she asked, unable to avoid the sarcasm.

"I happen to know where to go," he said.

Kody checked the rearview mirror now and then, but she couldn't tell if any of the cars she saw behind them were following her or not.

She was fairly certain she had gotten a call out—that she'd managed to dial Nick's number without Appleby noting what she was doing as they'd spoken. Then, of course, he'd made her leave her purse.

But he'd never looked at the phone. He didn't know what she had done…

If, of course, she had actually done it.

She had, she assured herself.

They passed the Miccosukee casino where lights were still bright and the parking lot abounded with cars.

Then, as they continued west, there were almost no cars.

Businesses advertising airboat rides seemed to creep up on them. The lights were low and the darkness out there at night seemed almost surreal.

Kody had been driving nearly an hour when Appleby picked up his phone.

"My parents?" she asked.

"Yes, Miss Cameron. I'm making sure they'll be just fine."

Someone answered on the other end.

"Everything is good," he said. And he smiled at Kody and hung up. "Just keep on helping me and we'll be fine."

"You need more than just me," she said. "This is the kind of project you need a host of workers to accomplish. We have to find the pilings. We think we know that he buried the stash at the corner of the main chickee, but we're not sure. And how deep? Exactly where? We need more people to look."

"Maybe," he told her.

"Just how many friends do you have? And do you really trust these people? Okay, so I've seen you in action. You extorted an airboat from people who were forced to help you. But remember, people you bribe and threaten just might want to bite back, you know," Kody told him.

"Would you bite back?" he asked her.

"If you keep threatening my parents, I promise you, I'll bite back!"

"Not if you want them alive. And slow down!"

Kody slowed down. She had no idea what he was looking for. If she were to turn to the right at the moment, she'd wind up in a canal. Not a pleasant thought. If she turned to the left, as far as she could see, there was nothing but soupy marsh. They were, she knew, near Shark Valley, but it was still ahead of them on the trail by a mile or two.

"Here," he said.

"Where's 'here'?" Kody demanded.

"Slow down!"

She slowed even more and glanced in the rearview mirror.

There were no lights behind them.

She wasn't being followed. Her heart seemed to sink.

"Right there!" Appleby told her. "See there? See the road? And don't get any ideas. You sink us in a canal or a bog out here, your parents die. Oh, and you die, too. So, drive, and drive carefully."

"Do you know how pitch-dark it is out here?" Kody demanded.

"Do you know that's why they give cars bright lights?" Appleby retorted.

Kody grated her teeth. She turned to the left and slowly, carefully, followed the dirt road Appleby had indicated. It seemed to head into nothing but dense green grass and it slowly disappeared.

"That's good," Appleby said. "Here. This is fine. It's as far as we go by car, my dear."

She's already been dragged through the swamp. She'd spent a night in a chickee. She'd walked, not knowing if she'd disturb a rattler or a coral snake, or if she'd step on a log that turned out to be an alligator. She shouldn't have been so terrified.

And yet she was.

Appleby shoved his gun into his waistband and tossed her a backpack. "Get your flashlight," he commanded her.

She found a large flashlight in the pack along with water, a folded shovel, a pick and a power bar.

They might have been on a planned hike or tour into the wilderness!

"Turn your light on," he said.

She did so, as did he. The flashlights illuminated great circles of brush and grass and trees. "There," he said.

Where?

And then she saw an airboat before them.

"Let's go!" he said.

She took a step; the ground was no longer solid.

She stepped into swamp and prayed she wasn't disturbing a cottonmouth.

It was only a few steps to the airboat. She was grateful to climb aboard it.

And then Appleby was with her, the motor was revving and they were moving deeper into the abyss of the night.

"I WILL BE there when they arrive," Jason Tiger assured Nick. "I'll have Miccosukee police with me. They know how to hide in the night. We'll be on it, I promise."

"But don't approach until we're out there," Nick said. "We're trying to find her parents. We'll be behind them. We have a ranger meeting us to take us out to the hammock. We'll take the first miles by airboat and then switch to canoes so that we're not heard."

"We won't approach. Unless, of course, we see that Miss Cameron is in imminent danger."

"Of course," Nick agreed.

Nick spoke with Tiger as he waited for Craig to join him. He hung up just as his teammate joined him in the car.

"You know, I keep thinking about this," Nick said.

"We haven't thought of anything but for days now," Craig said grimly.

"No. I mean the timing. I went to Kody's house at 8:00 p.m. Her mom and dad were still out—at a board meeting. We came to the hotel. We were at the hotel about three hours or so. That would mean that Appleby got to her house, either charmed or laid a trap for her parents when they returned, and then found someone to threaten who had a boat, and got Kody's mom and dad out on the boat. At least, that's what he told Kody."

"And?" Craig asked him. "Ah. Yeah, timing. You don't think that he really got them out on a boat. We have the Coast Guard out, but, of course, there are so many boats out there. And they can search for the Cameron couple. Thing is..."

"There are hundreds of boats out on the water. It's dark, and the bay stretches forever, and boats move," Nick said. He shook his head. "But I don't think they're on a boat."

"Where do you think they are?"

"Somewhere near the house," Nick said. "I can't look, though. I have to get out there. I have to get out there as quickly as possible. I know what Kody was doing, where she was looking, what she believed. I need—"

"To be there. I get it. Drop me at the Cameron house.

I'll find her parents, if they are anywhere near the house," Craig said firmly.

Nick nodded. "Thank you."

"It's a plan, my friend. It's a good plan. I'll get some help out to the house with me. If Mr. and Mrs. Cameron are anywhere near, we'll find them. And, if they're on the water, the Coast Guard will find them. Appleby knows Kody. He knows that she'll do anything he says as long as she's worried about her parents."

"We're ahead of him by one step this time," Nick said. "He didn't know that she got a call through on her phone, that I heard what went on between them. As far as he knows, we don't have a clue that Kody has been taken, that he has her out in the Everglades."

"She's really the right stuff," Craig said lightly.

She's perfect! Nick thought, and it felt as if the blood burned in his veins.

He knew he probably shouldn't be on the case now. Because he would kill, he would die, to see that she was safe. And that was just the way it was.

Chapter Ten

The airboat drifted onto the marshy land just before the rise of the hammock.

Kody's heart sank when she thought about the impossibility of the task before them. People had known about the Anthony Green stash forever. Scholars had mused and pondered on it.

They'd agreed that the treasure was in the Everglades.

Where bodies and more had disappeared since the coming of man.

"Get your pack. We'll head straight back," Appleby told her. "That bastard G-man had it down right, just before everything went to hell, before your silly friend freaked out and ran. You know, this could have all been over. We could have found the treasure. I'd have left you out here, where one of those rangers or Miccosukee police would have found you.

"Yep. It could have all been over. You know, letting that man in was the only mistake I made," Appleby said, and shrugged. "He talked a good story—he pulled it off. He acted as if he could be tough when needed."

He grinned at Kody. "Maybe that's why you two hit it off so well. Two actors, cast in different roles in life."

Appleby laughed, amused by his observation. "Okay, let's go. Get back there. We're going to find the site of the pilings, and we're going to start digging."

"Don't you think that this is a little crazy?" Kody asked him. "The local police know that you were here, the FBI know that you were here…they'll have someone out here."

"Why would they have someone out here?"

"It was a crime scene!"

Appleby laughed. "They looked for me here. They didn't find me here. They've moved on. They're checking the airlines and private planes. They're going to be certain that I've fled the area. They won't be looking for me here. So let's get started."

"This is ridiculous. It's dark. I can step on a snake. You can step on a snake. I saw gator holes back there. You could piss off a gator—"

"Yep. So let's hurry. Over here. That's where your lover boy seemed to be when all hell broke loose. And he was going by your determination."

It was insane. Maybe by daylight. Maybe with a dozen people digging and working…

"It could be worse," Appleby said.

"Really?"

"It could be summer." Appleby laughed and swatted his neck. "If it was summer, the mosquitos would be unbearable."

Every step in the night was torture. At least, once

they had moved in from the edges of the hammock, the ground was sturdy, a true limestone shelf.

It was difficult to get a bearing in the darkness. While the stars remained in the sky, the glow of the flashlights only illuminated circles of light; large, yes, but not large enough. She heard the chirping of crickets and, now and then, something else. Something that slunk into the water from the land. Something that moved through the trees. There were wild boars out here, she knew. Dangerous creatures if threatened. There were Florida panthers, too. Horribly endangered, and yet, if one was there, and threatened…

She kept walking, searching the ground, a sense of panic beginning to rise within her as she thought about the hopelessness of what she was doing. And then she came upon an indentation in the earth. She paused and shone her light down.

The dry area of the heavy pine piling would have eroded with time. But beneath the limestone and far into the water, the wood had been preserved.

She'd found it.

A piling that indicated the corner of the main chickee where, decades ago, Anthony Green had maintained the Everglades "office" for his illicit distillery.

She looked up; Appleby was staring at her.

"Time to dig!"

"WE'VE BEEN WATCHING HER. She has been safe," Jason Tiger told Nick. "You don't see them, but there are three men with me, watching from different angles. Oliver Osceola is in a tree over there—he's closest.

Appleby has kept his gun out, so we've been exceptionally careful not to be seen or to startle him in any way." He was quiet for a minute. "We have a sniper. A good one. David Cypress served three tours of duty in the Middle East. If we need—"

"We need to keep watching now. My partner is searching for Kody Cameron's parents. She'll throw herself in front of him, if she's worried about what will happen to her folks." The burning sensation remained with Nick, something that he fought—reminding himself over and over again that he was a federal agent, responsible to his calling. He would make every move the way a federal agent would—and that included killing Appleby point-blank if necessary to save a civilian.

The time taken to reach the hammock deep in the Everglades behind Shark Valley had seemed to be a lifetime.

He was here now.

He could see Appleby and Kody.

"All right, we're ready," Jason Tiger said. "You call the shots."

Nick nodded and ducked low into the grass. He kept as close to the ground as he could, making his way around to the area where Kody and Appleby were standing. He came close enough to hear them speaking.

"That's it! Now dig. It's there somewhere! You see! Ah, you were such a doubter, Miss Cameron! Dig! We have found it."

Kody was trying to assemble a foldable spade.

"You need to make a phone call," she said.

"I need you to dig."

"Make the call. It's been an hour again. I mean it—make the call."

"What if I just cut you up a little bit, Miss Cameron?"

"Then you'd have to dig yourself," Kody told him. "Make the call."

"You want me to make a call? Fine, I'll make a call."

Appleby pulled out his phone. He placed a call. He appeared to be speaking to someone.

But Nick wondered if there was actually anyone on the other end.

Had the man really taken Kody's parents out on a boat somewhere? Did he have new accomplices watching over them, actually ready to kill?

Or had Nick been right? Were they somewhere near their own home?

Still a safe distance, hunkered low in the rich grasses, Nick put a call through to Craig. "Anything yet?"

"No. But we have search-and-rescue dogs on the way. We're going to find them. What's going on at your end? Have you found Kody and Appleby?"

"We have them. Jason Tiger has had them in sight. We're good here. Just…just find Kody's parents."

As he spoke he heard the dogs start to bay. They were on to something. He suddenly found himself praying that Craig and the men and the dogs weren't going to find corpses. The corpses of two people he had never met.

"Bones," Craig said over the phone.

"Bones?"

"And a little gravestone. For JoJo, a little dog who died about a decade ago."

"Oh, lord. Craig—"

"Hold up. We've got something. The dogs are heading across the street. There's a park over there. I think he has them in the park, Nick. Right back with you!"

KODY DIDN'T TRUST APPLEBY. She knew the man really didn't care if people lived or died.

She wondered with a terrible, sinking feeling if her parents weren't already dead. If Appleby hadn't come into the house, waited for them and shot them down in cold blood…

"I want to talk to my mother," she said.

"What?"

"I want to talk to my mother. I want to know that she's alive. I don't believe you and I don't trust you. And this is sick and ridiculous, and if I'm going to continue to search and help you, I want to know that my mother is alive!" Kody said determinedly.

"Do you know what I could do, little girl?" Appleby asked her. "Do you have any idea of what I could do to you? Let me describe a few possibilities. Your kneecaps. You can't imagine the pain of having your kneecap shot out. I could shoot them both—and then leave you here. Eventually birds of prey and other creatures would come along and then the fun would really start. They would eat you alive. Slowly. They're very fond of soft tissue, especially birds of prey. They love to pluck out eyes…you can't begin to imagine. With any luck, you'd be dead by then."

Kody wasn't about to be swayed. "I want to talk to my mother."

"You can't talk to your mother."

"Why not? Is she dead? If she's dead, I don't give a damn what you do to me."

"She can't talk because there isn't anyone with her to hand her a phone!"

"I thought she was being held on a boat by people who would kill her."

"She's alive and well, Kody. Okay, maybe not so *well*, but she is alive. She's just tied up at the moment."

"Tied up where?"

"Does it matter? She can't talk right now." Appleby let out a growl of aggravation. "She can't talk. I knocked them out, left them tied up. They're alive, Kody."

"How do I trust you?"

"How do you not? You don't have a choice. Start moving. The longer you take, the more danger there is for your mom and dad."

"Maybe you've never even had them!" Kody said.

Appleby grinned. "Mom. Her name is Elizabeth, nickname Beth. She's about five feet, six inches. A pretty brunette with short, bobbed hair. Dad—Daniel. Six-two, blue eyes, graying dark hair. Yep, not to worry, Kody, dear, I do know the folks."

Kody managed to snap her shovel into working condition. For a moment she stared at Appleby, then she studied the ground and jumped back.

"What?" Appleby demanded.

"Snake."

"It will move."

"Yes, I'm trying to let it. It's a very big snake."

"It's just a ball python," Appleby said. "Someone's pet they let loose out here. Damn, but I hate that! People being so irresponsible. They've ruined the ecosystem."

Kody stared at him. He hadn't minded shooting an accomplice at close range. But he was worried about the ecosystem.

Thankfully, the snake at her feet was a non-native constrictor instead of a viper.

She swallowed hard.

The snake was gone.

She started to dig.

"TELL ME YOU'VE got something!" Nick whispered to Craig.

"Yes! We've got them. They were left under the bridge at the edge of the park. They couldn't twist or turn a lot or they'd have been in a canal. But we have them. We have them both. Elizabeth and Daniel Cameron are safe."

"Roger that. Thank you," Nick said. He clicked the phone closed, then inched through the grass and rose slightly, giving a signal to Jason Tiger to hold for his cue.

Kody suddenly let out a little cry, stepping backward.

"What?" Appleby demanded.

"Another snake…it's a coral snake. A little coral snake, but they can be really dangerous."

"No, that's not a coral snake. It's just a rat snake. Rat snakes are not poisonous."

"'Red touch yellow, kill a fellow. Black touch yellow, friend of Jack,'" Kody said, quoting the age-old way children were taught to recognize coral snakes from their non-venomous cousins.

"Yeah! Look, black on yellow!" Appleby said.

"No, red is touching yellow!"

"You want to get your nose down there and check?" he demanded.

"I am not touching that snake!" Kody said.

Appleby made a move. Nick could judge the man's body motion, the way that he crouched. He was getting ready to strike out.

And that was it.

Nick went flying across the remaining distance between them.

Appleby spun around, but he never knew Nick was coming, never saw what hit him. Nick head-butted the man, bringing him down to the ground.

The man's gun went flying.

They could all hear the popping sound as it was sucked into the swamp.

Appleby made no effort to struggle. Nick had raised a fist; Appleby just stared at him. He started to laugh. "You won't do it, will you? Pansy lawman. You won't do it. In fact…"

Nick didn't listen to the rest; he was already rising. Jason Tiger and his men were coming in to take the prisoner.

He looked over at Kody, who was standing there,

shaking. She hadn't moved from her position; she was just staring at him.

Then she flew at him, her fists banging against his chest. "Nick! You idiot, he has my mom and dad. He's going to kill my mom and dad. He'll never tell us—"

"That's right! They'll die!" Appleby chortled.

Nick caught Kody's hands. He turned and glanced at Appleby. "No, actually, Dan and Beth are just fine. They're being checked out at Mercy Hospital as we speak, but I imagine they'll be home by the time Kody and I manage to get back in."

Kody went limp, falling against him. "Really?"

"Really," he said.

He started to lead her back toward the police boat that had brought him to the hammock.

"Thank you!" she whispered.

"You did it, you know. Getting the call through. If you hadn't managed that, no one would have known. You did it, Kody."

She looked up at him. "I called the right guy, huh?" she said softly.

He kissed her lightly, holding her close, and heedless of who might see.

Appleby let out a horrendous scream. "It got me! It got me! Son of a bitch, it got me! Help, you've got to get me help, fast. You have to slice it, suck the poison out… It got me. You bastards, do something!"

"Oh, I don't know," Jason Tiger said. "David, did you see the snake?"

"Had to be a rat snake."

With Appleby supported between them, Jason

Tiger and David Cypress walked by them. Jason Tiger winked. *Rat snake*, he mouthed to Nick.

And Nick grinned.

Yep…

Let Appleby do a little wondering, after what he had done to others.

The winter's night was nearly over. Morning's light was on the way. And with it, Nick felt, all good things.

It was done. Case over, the way he liked it.

Appleby would rot beyond bars.

And Kody was safe, in his arms.

"'He hath, my lord, of late made many tenders of his affection to me!'"

Beyond a doubt, Dakota Cameron made the most stunning Ophelia that Nick had ever seen.

The play was definitely different; not that, until now, he'd really been an expert on plays.

He was learning.

But even with what he knew, *Hamlet Thus They Say* was a different kind of show. Of course, Kody was beyond stupendous and Nick could hear the buzz among the people around him.

It was going to be a hit.

There was no real curtain call; the play just continued for four hours each night. There was no intermission. It was "living theater."

And it was FBI night.

Craig was there with Kieran. Mike, Craig's partner, was there. Nick had been glad to learn that he would be repartnered with Sherri Haskell, and she was there with her New York City cop husband, Mo.

Director Egan had even come out for the night.

They waited in front of the theater for the last of the attendees to leave.

"I can't believe that they didn't break character—not once!" Kieran said, smiling at Nick. "Okay, so, actually, I can't believe you disappear, Kody goes home to settle some things, and you come back a duo, having caught a man who held a spot on the Ten Most Wanted list—and found a treasure that's been missing for decades."

"Ah, but we didn't find the treasure!" Nick told her.

"I think you did."

Nick laughed softly, looking at Craig. "Poor Ophelia, going mad for love! I think Craig and I did a bit of the same. The county, the federal government and the Miccosukee Tribe all got together—and that's when they found the treasure. None of us stayed because, as we know, the FBI is a commitment—and because the show must go on. That's a commitment for Kody.

"We stayed in Miami just long enough for her to spend a day with her parents. Then we all had to be back up here. But, yes, Kody's research and logic led those forces to the stash. They had to dig pretty deep. I don't think that Nathan Appleby would have managed to get it all out. He might have found some pieces, though. It had been buried in leather cases, and they were coming apart. But, yes, the stash was filled with gold pieces—South African—and emeralds, diamonds, you name it."

“What will happen with it all?” Kieran asked.

“I understand some of the pieces will wind up in a museum. Some will go to the state and some will wind up helping to keep the Crystal Manor going. It will be part of the trust that runs the place—along with Kody’s family. And speaking of Kody’s family…” He paused, waving as Daniel and Beth Cameron exited the theater. Nick drew them over and introduced them to those in their group they hadn’t met already.

Of course, on arrival in the city, they’d been brought to Finnegan’s and feted with stout from excellent taps and the world’s best shepherd’s pie.

“Wow. And you’re FBI, too?” Daniel asked Sherri.

“Yes, sir. I am.”

“Well, our girl will be hanging around with a good crowd,” Daniel told his wife.

“Yes, certainly,” Beth Cameron said, but she looked a little puzzled.

“Is anything wrong?” Nick asked her.

“No, no, of course not. I’m not so sure that I get it. I mean, living theater, or whatever it is. I’m used to the actors just…acting on stage. I’ve never talked with the actors before during a performance,” she said. “But, of course, Kody and Kevin were wonderful!”

Kieran laughed. “Yes, they were. They were both wonderful.”

“She talked to me—but as if she didn’t know me!” Daniel said.

“Well, she doesn’t know you. Not as Ophelia,” Nick explained.

“Yes, yes, of course. She’s playing a role. I guess.

I mean, of course. It's just strange," Beth said. She sighed. "She has a beautiful voice. Maybe it will be a musical next. Oh, look!" she murmured, catching Nick by the hand. "There—do you know who that is?"

Nick looked. No, he didn't.

"That's Mayor Holden Burke. With his little boy, Adrian. And his wife, Monica."

The man, next to the boy who appeared to be about nine, noted Beth just as she was whispering about him.

He waved and came over, catching the hands of his wife and son so they would join him. Adrian Burke was carrying a large bouquet of flowers.

Beth introduced people all around.

"We're so grateful," he said, and his wife nodded, looking around. "You're the agents who were involved?"

"Craig and I were down there," Nick said. "But, like I said in my debriefing, in all honesty, Kody was the one who got Nathan Appleby to say where Adrian was being held. And an agent down in South Florida, Jason Tiger, got the information back to the city."

The cast door opened and the actors were all coming out. There was a round of applause that sounded up and down the street.

Nick saw Kody, and saw that she was searching through the crowd.

Looking for him, he thought. He waved and then watched her chat and smile with grace and courtesy as she spoke to fans and signed programs.

"Excuse us," Mayor Burke said.

Nick realized, as the mayor and his family approached Kody, that she'd never actually met them.

She took the flowers from Adrian, hugged him and planted a kiss on his cheek. She was hugged by the mayor and his wife.

The three left then, waving to the others.

And, finally, the crowd around the performers had just about thinned out.

He, Kody's parents, the Finnegans and the extended FBI family made their way over to the group, congratulating the actors. Nick bypassed everyone, going directly to Kody and taking her in his arms.

Her kiss was magnificent. Her eyes touched his with promise. She was filled with the excitement and adrenaline of opening night; she was also anxious, he knew, for their time together.

But first, of course, they all made their way to Finnegan's for a late-night supper and a phenomenal Irish band.

And, at last, it was time for him and Kody to leave.

In his company car they saw her parents to their hotel in midtown. Then they headed for his apartment.

When they'd first returned to the city a few weeks ago, they'd kept both apartments. That had proved to be a total waste. They both worked, and worked hard, but their free time was spent together.

When a night bartender at Finnegan's was about to lose his lease—his apartments were being turned into condos—Kody offered her apartment to him, and so, just last week, she had made the official move into Nick's place.

It was simply the best accommodation: a full bedroom, an office, a parlor, two baths. Plus it was situated right on the subway line that connected Finnegan's and the FBI offices and midtown.

Kody, of course, had already made some changes, and Nick loved them.

There were posters on the wall—show posters and band posters—and there was artwork, as well. Seascapes, mostly, from Florida, and paintings from New York City, too.

One of his favorite pieces they had bought together down in the Village. It was a signed painting of the Brooklyn Bridge.

"A new artist—who will be a famous artist one day," Kody had said. "And if not, it's still a brilliant painting and I love it."

She was, he thought, everything he needed.

Life, as he saw it, was too often grim. But Kody looked for the best, always. And she saw the best that way. She showed it to him, as well.

"So, what did you think of the play? What did you really think?" she asked when they stepped into the apartment, alone at last.

"I loved it," he said.

"Really?"

"I really did. But I do believe you have to have the right cast for that kind of theater. Your cast is truly amazing. Powerful performers—they all engaged the audience."

"I don't think my mom saw it that way."

Nick laughed. "She admitted to a bit of confusion."

"But you really thought that it was good?" she asked.

"I, like the critics, raved!"

She flew into his arms, kissing him. "Are you a liar?" she asked.

"No!"

She laughed. "Doesn't matter," she said. "You were there for me, on FBI night."

"I'll come to the show whenever I can."

"You don't have to. It's okay. We'll settle in and we'll figure it all out—the time, the FBI, the theater..."

"I know we will," he told her. And he kissed her again, shrugging out of his jacket as he did so. It had been a chilly night. Kody was in a heavy wool coat and it, too, hit the floor.

She kicked off her shoes, their lips never parting.

Nick suddenly dipped low and swept her off her feet. She laughed as she looked up at him.

"It's been a dramatic night. Thought I should be dramatic, too."

"You really are quite the actor. You know, down in Florida when I first saw you, I really thought you were a bad guy."

"But not really. You said you knew I wasn't a killer."

"You played the part very well."

"Thank you. If the law-enforcement thing fails..."

She touched his face gently, studying his eyes. "It won't. You love what you do, and you're very good, and I would never want anything different for you."

"Nor would I change a thing about you," he told her huskily.

She smiled.

They headed into the bedroom and Nick laid Kody carefully upon the sheets, kneeling beside her. He kissed her lips again, but she was impatient and rose against him, crawling over him, straddling him, while she tore away her clothes.

"Ah, my lady! Wait, I have a surprise for you," he said.

She laughed softly. "And I have a surprise for you! I can wait for nothing." And she shoved him down. She lay against him, teased his shoulders, chest and abdomen with her kisses as she tugged at his clothing, entangled them both in it, and laughed as they finally managed to strip down completely. She whispered to him, touching him, making love to him with a combination of tenderness and fierceness that drove him wild.

It was later, much later, when he lay sated and incredulous, cradling her to him, his chin atop her head, that she said, "You told me you had a surprise for me."

"Ah, yes!"

He got out of bed and Kody sat up to watch him, curious as he left the room.

He'd never been with an actress before.

This one, he knew he would love all his life. Therefore, he had figured, he would get it right.

He plucked the champagne from the refrigerator and prepared the ice bucket.

The plate of chocolate-covered strawberries was ready, as well.

Along with the long-stemmed roses. And a tiny box.

He swept up the bucket, the plate balanced atop it,

the roses in his mouth. And he walked back into the bedroom.

Kody cried out with delight, clapping her hands.

"Oh, but you are perfect! Perfect! Roses, chocolate-covered strawberries, champagne—and a naked FBI guy! What more could one want?"

They both burst into laughter.

And he joined her in the bed.

They popped the cork on the champagne, laughed as it spilled over. They shared the strawberries and Kody smelled the roses and looked at him seriously.

"I love you so much," she whispered. "Is it…is it all right to say that? I tend to speak quickly, rashly, sometimes. I mean…well, you know. I probably could have gotten myself or someone else killed back in Florida if you weren't you. If you hadn't been undercover. If—"

He pulled her into his arms. "I wouldn't have you any other way at all. I love that you said what you did. I love you. And…"

He realized he was terribly nervous. He might be a well-trained agent, but his fingers were trembling as he reached for the little box.

Kody took the box, her eyes on his. She opened it and stared in silence.

His heart sank. "It's too soon, too much," he murmured. "I—"

She threw her arms around him, and kissed him, and kissed him, and kissed him.

"Is that a yes?"

"Yes!" She laughed. "Not even I am that good an actress!"

He took the ring and slipped it on her finger. “Since we’re living in sin…?”

“This kind of love could never be a sin,” she assured him.

“You’re really so beautiful…in every way,” he told her.

She smiled—a mischievous smile. “With the pick-up line you gave me in Florida, who would have thought that we would wind up here!”

“Go figure,” he agreed.

He kissed her and lay her back on the bed.

“Go figure,” he repeated.

And he started kissing her again and again…

It was, after all, opening night. For the show.

And for the rest of their lives.

* * * * *

Keep reading for a special preview of
the next novel from
New York Times *bestselling author*
Heather Graham
A PERFECT OBSESSION
The second thrilling story in the
NEW YORK CONFIDENTIAL *series.*
Coming soon from MIRA Books.

Chapter One

"Horrible! Oh, God, horrible—tragic!" John Shaw said, shaking his head with a dazed look as he sat on his bar stool at Finnegan's Pub.

Kieran nodded sympathetically. Construction crews had found old graves when they were working on the foundations at the hot new downtown venue Le Club Vampyre.

Anthropologists had found the new body among the old graves the next day.

It wasn't just *any* body.

It was the body of supermodel Jeannette Gilbert.

Finding the old graves wasn't much of a shock—not in New York City, and not in a building that was close to two centuries old. The structure that housed Le Club Vampyre was a deconsecrated Episcopal church. The church's congregation had moved to a facility it had purchased from the Catholic church—whose congregation was now in a sparkling new basilica over on Park Avenue. While many had bemoaned the fact that such a venerable old institution had been turned into an establishment for those into sex, drugs, and rock and roll, life—and business—went on.

And with life going on…

Well, work on the building's foundations went on, too.

It was while investigators were still being called in following the discovery of the newly deceased body—moments before it hit the news—that Kieran Finnegan learned about it, and that was because she was helping out at her family's establishment, Finnegan's on Broadway. Like the old church/nightclub behind it, Finnegan's dated back to just before the Civil War, and had been a pub for most of those years. Since it was geographically the closest place to the church with liquor, it had apparently seemed the right spot at that moment for Professor John Shaw. They'd barely opened; it was still morning, and it was a Friday, and Kieran was only there at that time because her bosses had decided on a day off following their participation in a lengthy trial. She'd just come up from the cellar, fetching a few bottles of a vintage chardonnay for her brother that had been ordered specifically for a lunch that day, when John Shaw had caught her attention, desperate to talk.

"I can't tell you how excited I was, being called in as an expert on a find like that," the professor told Kieran. "They both wanted me! By they, I mean Henry Willoughby, president of Preserve our Past, and Roger Gleason, owner and manager of the club. I was so honored. It was exciting to think of finding the *old* bodies—not the new body. But then…opening a decaying coffin and finding Jeannette Gilbert! And the university was entirely behind me, allowing me the time to be at my site, giving me a chance to bring my grad students here. Oh, my God! I found her! Oh, it was…"

John Shaw was shaking as he spoke. He was a man who'd seen all kinds of antiquated horrors, an expert in the past. He fit the stereotype of an academic with his lean physique, his thatch of wild white hair and his little gold-framed glasses. He held doctorate degrees in archaeology and anthropology, and science and history meant everything to him.

Kieran realized that he'd been about to say once again that it was horrible, like nothing he'd ever experienced. He clearly realized that he was speaking about a recently living woman, adored by adolescent boys and heterosexual males of all ages—a woman who was going to be deeply mourned.

Jeannette Gilbert. Media princess. The model and actress had disappeared two weeks ago after the launch party for a new cosmetics line. Her agent and manager, Oswald Martin, had gone on the news, begging kidnappers for her safe return.

At that time, no one knew if she actually *had* been kidnapped. One reporter speculated that she'd disappeared on purpose, determined to get away from the very man begging kidnappers for her release: her agent and manager.

Kieran hadn't really paid much attention; she'd assumed that the young woman—who'd been made famous by the same Oswald Martin—had just had enough of being adored and fawned over and told what to do at every move, and she'd decided to take a hiatus.

Or it might have been some kind of publicity gig; her disappearance had certainly ruled the headlines. There were always tabloid pictures of Jeannette with this or that man, and then speculation in the same tabloids that her manager had furiously burst into a hotel room, sending Jeannette Gilbert's latest lover—gold digger, as Martin referred to any young man she dated—flying out the door.

In the past few weeks the "celebrity" magazines had run rampant with rumors of a mystery man in her life. A secret love. Kieran knew that only because her twin brother, Kevin, was an actor—struggling his way into TV, movies and theater. He read the tabloids avidly, telling Kieran that he was "reading between the lines," and being up on what was going on was critical to his career. There were too many actors—even good ones!—out there and too few roles. Any edge was a good edge.

While all the speculation had been going on, Kieran couldn't help wondering if Jeannette's secret lover had killed her—or if, maybe, her steel-handed manager had done so.

Or, since this was New York City with a population in the millions, it was possible that some deranged person had murdered her. Perhaps this person felt that if she was relieved of her life, she'd be out of the misery caused by being such a beautiful, glittering star, always the focus of attention.

It was fine to speculate when you believed that someone was just pulling a major publicity stunt.

Now Kieran felt bad, of course. From what she *knew*

now, it seemed evident that the woman had indeed been murdered.

Not that she had any of the facts other than that Jeannette had been found in the bowels of the earth in a nineteenth-century tomb, but it was unlikely that Jeannette Gilbert had crawled into a historic coffin in a lost catacomb to die of natural causes.

"It was so horrible!" John Shaw repeated woefully. "When we found her, we just stared. One of my silly young grad students screamed, and she wasn't the only one. We called the police immediately. The club wasn't open then, of course—except to us, those of us who were working. I was there for hours while they grilled me. And now…now, I need this!" His hand shook as he picked up his double shot of single-malt scotch to swallow in a gulp.

He was usually a beer man. Ultra light.

It was horrible, yes, as Shaw kept saying. But, of course, he realized he'd be in the news, interviewed for dozens of papers and magazines and television, as well.

After all…

He'd been the one to find Jeannette Gilbert dead. In a coffin, in a deconsecrated church now turned into the Le Club Vampyre. Well, that was news.

The pub would soon be buzzing, especially since it was on the other side of the block from Le Club Vampyre.

The whole situation, aside from the grief of a young woman's untimely death, was interesting to Kieran. In her "real" job during the week she worked as a psychologist and therapist for psychiatrists Bentley Fuller and

Allison Miro. But, like her brothers, she often filled in at the pub; it was kind of a home away from home for them all. The pub had been in the family—belonging to a distant great-great uncle—from the mid–nineteenth century. Her own parents were gone now, and that made the pub even more precious to her and her older brother, Declan, her twin, Kevin, and her "baby" brother, Daniel.

So, while Declan actually managed the pub and made it his life's work, Kieran was employed by doctors Fuller and Miro, Kevin pursued his acting career and Danny strove to become the city's best tour guide. And they all spent a great deal of time at Finnegan's.

The tragic death of Jeannette Gilbert would soon have all their patrons gossiping about this latest outrage regarding Le Club Vampyre. They'd been talking about it now and then for six months, ever since the sale of the old church to Dark Doors Incorporated. Patrons had become extremely glum when the club had opened a month ago. A club! Like that! In an old church!

The club had also, of course, been the main topic of conversation yesterday, when the news had come out that unknown gravesites had been found—and Professor John Shaw had been called in.

Of course, people were still talking about the old catacombs today. Not that finding graves while digging in foundations was unusual in New York. It was just creepy-cool enough.

Creepy-cool was fine when you were talking about very old gravesites.

Because they were old—they were the site of

the earthly remains of people who'd lived and died long ago.

Not the newly deceased.

At the moment, though, Kieran was one of the few people who knew that the body of Jeannette Gilbert had been discovered. Kieran had been among the first to find out; that was because she knew Dr. John Shaw—professor of archaeology and anthropology at NYU, famed in academic circles for his work on sites from Jamestown, Virginia, to Beijing, China—very well. He and a group of his colleagues had met at Finnegan's Pub one night a month as long as she could remember.

When she'd see him looking so distressed, she'd ushered him into one of the small booths against the wall that divided the pub's general area from the offices. She'd gotten him his scotch—and she'd sat down with him so she could try to calm him down.

"Oh, my God! I can just imagine when it hits the news!" he said, looking at her with stricken eyes. And yet, she recognized a bit of awe in them…

Of course, he hadn't known Jeannette Gilbert. Kieran hadn't, either. She'd seen her once, on a red carpet, heading to the premiere of a new movie in a theater near Times Square.

Sadly, Jeannette hadn't been an especially talented actress. But she'd been too beautiful for most people to care.

"I'm so sorry you're the one who found her," Kieran said. That should've been the right thing to say; usually, people didn't want to find others dead. Though

John Shaw was going to be famous in the pop-culture world now, as well as the academic world.

But it was obvious that he was badly shaken.

He was accustomed to studying bones and mummies—not a woman who'd been recently murdered.

"I was—I am!—very excited about the project. I don't understand how the church could have lost all those graves. Can you imagine? Okay, so, you know how they built St. Paul's to accommodate folks farther north of Trinity back in the day? Well, they built St. Augustine's for those a little north of St. Paul's. And, according to my research so far, the church was fine until about 1860, when way too many people went off to fight in the Civil War. It wasn't deconsecrated—just more or less abandoned because the congregations were so much smaller. Then, according to records, Father O'Hara passed away, and it took the church forever to send out a new priest. Apparently, there was structural damage by then, which closed off that section of the catacombs. You see, there was, until about seventy-five years ago, an entrance to the catacombs from the street, and I suppose everyone—church officials, city organizers, engineers, what have you—believed all the graves had been removed. Of course, most of the dead were buried then in wooden coffins, and in the ground area outside, most of those became dirt and bone. But there were underground catacombs, too. Coffins set upon shelves… Some of the dead were just shrouded, but some were in old wooden coffins, and they were decaying and falling apart and I had workers taking them down so carefully—and then there she was!"

He sipped his scotch again and looked at her intently. "Kieran, you're not to say a word, not yet. The police...they asked me not to speak about this until... until someone was notified. I don't think either of her parents are living, but she must have family..." His voice trailed off. "My God. It was ghastly!" he said a moment later. "Gruesome—ghastly!"

This time, he didn't sip his scotch. He swallowed it down in a gulp.

Kieran wasn't sure why she turned to look at the front door when she did; it was always opening and closing. Maybe she wanted to look anywhere except at John Shaw. She was a working psychologist, and yet she wasn't sure what to say to the man.

She glanced up just in time to see Craig Frasier come in and blink to adjust to the light.

She wasn't surprised Craig was there; they were seeing each other and had been since the affair over the "flawless" Capeletti diamond. They were talking about giving up their current situation, in which they each had dresser drawers at the other's apartment, and moving in together.

But while she had truly fallen in love with Craig, she was a little hesitant—and a little worried about the fact that the man she believed to be her soul mate also happened to be a special agent with the FBI. Her family was striving to be legitimate now, which hadn't always been the case. Growing up, her brothers had had a few brushes with the law.

And trusting her beloved brothers to behave wasn't easy. They were never malicious; however, their ways of helping friends out of bad situations weren't always the best.

Then again, she'd met Craig because of the Capeletti diamond and Danny's determination to do the right thing...

And because of some criminal clientele.

"Excuse me," she murmured to John, assuming that Craig had come to see her.

The door was still open; he stood in a pool of light and her heart leaped as she saw him. Craig was, in her mind, entirely impressive, tall and broad shouldered, with extraordinary eyes that seemed to take everything in.

But he had not, apparently, come to see her.

He greeted Kieran with a nod, held her shoulders for a minute—and then offered her a grim smile as he gently set her aside so he could move past her.

Something was up. Craig spent his free time here with her and her family. Her friends, coworkers and the usual clientele all knew that Craig and Kieran were a couple.

Today, however, there wasn't even a quick kiss. Craig was being very official.

He was heading straight to the booth where John Shaw was seated.

Kieran stood there for a minute, perplexed.

Of course, Craig was FBI. But a local woman had been killed, and no matter how famous she'd been, it should've remained a matter for the NYPD. And John Shaw had left the old church/screaming-hot nightclub less than an hour ago.

Why would Craig be here so quickly? And more to the point, why was the FBI involved?

She didn't get a chance to slide back into the booth and find out what was going on; she felt a tap on her shoulder and turned around.

Her brother Kevin was next to her. Kevin was a striking man—in *anyone's* opinion, she thought. He was tall and fit with fine features, dark red hair and deep blue eyes; their coloring was the same. They were twins, and it showed. She loved her brother and she felt that acting was the perfect career for him. Like all of them, however, he worked at the pub when he could.

"I have to talk to you!" he said urgently.

"Sure," she said.

"Not here. In the office," he told her. To her surprise, he glanced uneasily at Craig—whom he liked and with whom he was pretty good friends.

Her brother whirled her around and headed her down the entry aisle toward the bar and then to the left and down the hallway to the business office. He peered in, as if afraid their older brother might be there, since it was, basically, Declan's office.

He closed the door behind them.

"She's dead, Kieran! She's dead!" Kevin said, looking at her and shaking his head with dismay and anxiety.

She stared at him for a moment. He couldn't be talking about Jeannette Gilbert—no one knew she'd been found at the church yet, not according to John Shaw.

Her heart quaked with fear. She was afraid he was

talking about an old friend, or a longtime customer of the pub.

Someone he cared about deeply.

"Kevin, *who*?" she asked.

"Jeannette."

She frowned. "Jeannette Gilbert?"

He nodded.

"Okay," she said slowly. "*I* know that, because John Shaw just told me. But he only found her a few hours ago. The police asked him not to say anything."

Kevin took a deep breath. "Well, John Shaw might not have said anything, but one of the workers down there—a grunt? A student? I don't know—came out and told people on the street, and the story was picked up, and there are already media crews there."

She studied her brother. "Kevin, it's terrible. A young and beautiful young woman who was very popular has—I'm assuming—been murdered. But, Kevin, I'm afraid that terrible things do happen. But…we didn't know Jeannette Gilbert. Not personally."

"Yes," he said. "We did."

"We did?"

"*I* did," he corrected. "Kieran, I was the so-called 'mystery man' she was dating! I might have been the last one to see her alive."

The NYPD had been called in first; that was proper protocol, since New York City was where the body had been found.

Jeannette Gilbert hadn't been kidnapped in another state and subsequently killed in New York. She'd last been seen by her doorman entering her apartment; she was a longtime Manhattan resident. She had, in fact, grown up in Harlem, a little girl who'd lost both parents and gone on to live in a household filled with children and an aunt who hadn't wanted another mouth to feed.

At the age of seventeen, however, she had an affair with a rock star.

While the rock star denied any kind of intimate relationship with her at the time, he'd gone on to put her in one of his music videos soon after.

An agent had picked her up and it had been a classic tale—little girl lost had become a megastar. By twenty-five, she was gracing runways and doing cameo spots on television shows and even appearing in small roles in several movies. She was considered a true supernova.

Because Jeannette's physical appearance had been called *perfect* by every critic out there.

She could walk a runway.

She had beautiful skin, luscious hair, long legs and a body that didn't quit.

Craig Frasier had learned all this about Jeannette in the past few hours. Before that, she'd been a face he might have recognized on a magazine cover.

But he'd made it his business to read up on her quickly.

Because her death had suddenly become the focus of his life.

He'd been in his office, reading paperwork from witnesses about the murder of a known pimp, when he'd been summoned, along with his partner, Mike Dalton, to Assistant Director Richard Egan's office.

Craig and Mike had been partners for years. Craig had been assigned a young, new agent when Mike was laid up on medical—a shot to the buttocks—about a year ago. He'd learned then how much he appreciated his partner; they knew each other's minds. They naturally fell into a division of labor when it came to pounding the pavement and getting the inevitable paperwork done.

And there was no one Craig trusted more to have his back, especially in a shoot-out.

Egan, a good man himself, was hardcore Bureau. His personal life had suffered for it, but he never brought that into the office. He was the best kind of authority figure, as well—dignified, fair, compassionate. And efficient. He never wasted time. There were two chairs in front of his desk, but he hadn't waited for Craig and Mike to sit down. He'd started talking right away.

"I had a back-burner situation going on here," he'd told them. "We'd been given information, but the local police down in Fredericksburg, Virginia, were handling the case. A girl—a perfect-looking girl, an artist's model—disappeared about six months ago. A few weeks later, her body was found in a historic cemetery outside Fredericksburg. She'd been stabbed in the heart, then cleaned up, dressed up and laid out in a family mausoleum. She was discovered when the family's matriarch died, since she'd been put in the matriarch's space. As I said, it seemed to be a local matter, and the Fredericksburg police and Virginia state police had the murder. We were informed because of the unusual aspects."

Egan had paused, running his hands through his hair. Then he'd resumed speaking. "We're all aware of the high-profile disappearance of Jeannette Gilbert."

Mike had nodded. "Yeah, we were briefed with the cops about her disappearance when she went missing. We weren't really in on it, as you know. But we were on the lookout."

"Ms. Gilbert's been found. An archaeological dig at old St. Augustine's."

"You mean—" Mike began.

But Egan had cut him off. Yeah, he meant the new nightclub. Egan wasn't a fan. He'd gone on and ranted for a full minute about old historic places becoming nightclubs. In his opinion, that suggested New York City had no real respect for the past.

Craig knew Mike hadn't been asking his question because of the club; he'd been trying to ascertain if she'd been found dead.

Mike had glanced over at Craig; Craig shrugged.

They'd both just let Egan rant, figuring it was obvious. The poor girl was dead.

It had ended with Egan saying, "Yes, she's dead. And it is bizarre—as bizarre as that earlier case, maybe even more so. Because in this case, the perp had to know she'd be found quickly. He'd placed her in a historical site where anthropologists and archaeologists were expected to arrive imminently. Later, you can go over the info on the Virginia case, do some comparisons. We're part of the task force on this, but we're taking the lead, and you two are up for our division. Because, gentlemen, I believe we have a serial killer on our hands."

They'd asked about the security tapes.

Techs were going over those now.

"That's a bitch!" Egan had exclaimed. "Try looking for something out of the ordinary when every damned customer in the place is like an escapee from a Goth B flick or worse! Not to mention that the club closed down when the body was discovered. There's no club security at night other than the cameras, but cops have been patrolling the place since the historic folks stepped in."

From the office, he and Mike had gone straight to the church. The ME on duty was Anthony Andrews, a fine, detail-oriented doctor, but he hadn't really started yet.

Photographers were still taking pictures, trying to maintain the scene just as it had been after Professor Shaw had opened the first coffin—and had seen Jeannette Gilbert.

A half-dozen members of a forensic team had been moving around, but Dr. Andrews had delicately stopped the photo session to show Craig and Mike what he'd discovered. Gilbert had been killed in another location, stabbed through the heart, and then bathed and dressed and prepared before being placed in the old coffin.

Seeing her had been heartbreaking. He hadn't known the young woman or really anything about her until today, but she'd been young and beautiful and her life had been brutally taken. She lay in the old coffin, dressed in shimmering white, a wilted rose in her hands. With her eyes closed, it looked as if she slept.

Except, of course, she'd never wake again.

"Defensive wounds?" he'd asked Andrews.

"Not a one. She was taken by surprise. Whoever killed her stood close by—had to be someone who seemed trustworthy. Maybe someone she knew," the ME had speculated. "Or she could've had some kind of opiate in her system. Anyway, she didn't expect what was coming."

"Time of death?" Mike had asked. "She's been missing about two weeks."

"I'm thinking one to two weeks," Andrews had replied. "If she was abducted, perhaps soon after. And I don't believe she's been embalmed—but she was somehow preserved. Maybe in a freezer while he worked on her or made arrangements or..." He'd sighed. "I need to get her on the table."

Two patrol officers, the first on the scene, had closed off the area. Luckily, the club was closed, pending the investigation of the newly discovered crypt. Detective Larry McBride with the major crimes division had been the first to arrive. Craig and Mike had worked with him before. He was particularly mild mannered but he had a brilliant mind and nothing deterred his focus.

"Glad you guys are lead on this," McBride had told them. "This is... Well, I believe we definitely have a real psychopath on our hands. Bizarre! Wherever he killed her, he washed away the blood. I've got officers who'll be doing rounds with pictures of the dress. Pending notification of the so-called aunt who raised the girl, they'll be asking all her friends if she owned the dress, or if the killer obtained it."

"Checked the label," Andrews had said. "It's from Saks."

McBride had nodded. "Nice dress. She looks like a princess." He paused. "I have a daughter her age… So, anyway, no inside security by night—but cops watching on the street. The men on duty swore no one went in until Roger Gleason opened it up to wait for the archaeologists. Gleason says he comes in every day, even though the club's closed for a few days. I interviewed him and he seems to be on the up and up. Says he's personally not that interested in the historical stuff but seeing that the work goes well will actually make his club more famous. He's not one of those guys who lets his own property go unattended. He was working up here and heard Shaw's screams. Shaw swears there was no one down there at the time but him and a few of his grad students. I have names, et cetera, which I've emailed to you already. They were all questioned. I don't think they had anything to do with Ms. Gilbert's death. The mystery here is, *how the hell did the bastard get in with the body*? Anyway, the security footage is down at your office now. And, of course, we're hoping Forensics can come up with something. This killer…well, they're calling in shrinks. You know, profilers. The murder was cold, swift and brutal. But then he takes all this time with her. He comes in like a shadow—and then leaves her on display, waiting to be found. I talked with Egan, and I've been hanging around for you guys. Actually, I'm almost afraid to leave. It's a media frenzy out there."

By then the frenzy on the streets had involved more than just media. Word had spread; dozens of celebrity stalkers and those inclined to the macabre had congregated outside the club.

Craig had questioned Gleason himself before leaving. He seemed like a Wall Street type—and although his club might be Goth, he was far more prone to the elegant in his manner and dress.

New York City's finest were dealing with the facility and crowd control.

"I need to talk to Shaw," Craig had decided.

But Shaw wasn't there. They'd heard that when he'd first gotten up close and personal with the body, he'd screamed like a banshee.

And Allie Benoit, John Shaw's grad student and assistant, had told him that Shaw had spoken with the police, and then freaked out and fled. Allie was pretty sure he'd gone to the pub—the pub whose back wall abutted that of the old church-turned-nightclub.

And that *was* exactly what John Shaw had done.

Finnegan's!

Craig had sworn, walked around the corner and reached the pub.

The damned man just had to go to Finnegan's!

The pub had stood there almost as long as the church. It had seen the New York draft riots during the Civil War, and the violence of the Irish gangs that had once held huge sway in a city where immigrants poured in daily from around the world.

The pub had witnessed so much history.

Including the recent history of the diamond heist that had nearly cost Kieran Finnegan her life.

"She won't be involved!" he'd said firmly, speaking aloud.

But before he'd entered, he'd known, somewhere in his gut, that the die had already been cast.

Of all the pubs in all the world.

Finnegan's.

Chapter Two

As he'd entered the pub, Craig's attention was all for his search. With luck, Kieran would be at the office today or—

Naturally, she'd walked directly over to him.

And he hadn't been able to do what he wanted to do—tell her that she wasn't to have the least interaction with *anyone* connected to the murder.

He didn't have the right to make that kind of demand.

And since she was here, she might have already served John Shaw, and John Shaw would've talked to her…

At the moment, though, he needed Shaw. She'd understand that; he never had to explain himself or his intentions to Kieran.

She knew what he did for a living; he knew about her professional work for doctors Fuller and Miro. They respected each other's professions and discussed things when they could—or when the other might have a useful insight. Or when, as occasionally happened, they became involved in the same case.

Fuller and Miro worked with the police and the FBI. They often gave their opinion of a suspected criminal's state of mind or behavior.

They'd been involved, all four of them together, in a situation before—the so-called Diamond Affair.

But now…

He wanted to hold her and yet he couldn't; he was here professionally.

Even as he approached the booth where John Shaw was seated, he was still hating the fact that the church where Jeannette had been found was directly behind Finnegan's. He'd come to terms with being in love with Kieran—and the fact that she, too, dealt with criminals.

However, it was still difficult for him to accept that she was sometimes too quick to put herself in danger in defense of others.

Yes, it seemed to be a Casablanca *moment.*

Of all the old abandoned dug-out holes in Manhattan....

The damned catacombs just had to be close to Finnegan's!

Too close… This place was too close to where a young woman lay dead, where her body had been stashed with the bones of those long forgotten.

Craig knew John Shaw, and Shaw knew him; they'd met at the pub several times when Shaw had come for his professional meetings or get-togethers—or when he just wanted to sip one of his ultralight beers and chill.

"Craig!" John said, looking up at him with surprise. "I—oh, my. You're coming to see me. So I guess it should be Special Agent Frasier. Not Craig. Look, I'm not sure what else I can say to anyone. All I know is that we opened that coffin and…and there she was."

Craig slid into the booth and smiled at him. "You must be pretty rattled."

"Yes. You're here officially? The police told me not to say anything yet. They need to contact the poor girl's family. I mean, that's why you're here—coming to me and not Kieran, right?"

"Yes, John, this is official. The NYPD detectives are on the case, of course, but we're taking part, as well. We've put together a task force. This is a very high-profile murder."

John nodded, his white hair—something of a strange mullet cut—flapping beside his ears. His glasses slid down his nose with his effort and he pushed them back with his forefinger.

"Of course. This needs to be solved fast," John said. "But…" His expression grew even more perplexed. "I don't know how I can help anymore. I don't know how I can help, period. Professor Digby—Aldous Digby, one of my associates—and I were there, and three grad students. Oh, and two of the construction guys. The guys were watching—waiting to get back to work. I didn't let them touch the coffin. Nice guys, but, you know, that coffin might be two hundred years old—well, you need to have a delicate touch. And Ms. Gilbert. The second I saw her… I have to admit I screamed. I was rattled, as you said. But I made sure everyone got out. We did and then went up to the church, the—the club area, to wait for the police."

"Right. So there were seven of you. I have the

names," Craig said. He was certain that the meticulous Detective McBride had sent his email.

He'd also seen Jeannette Gilbert's body at the site.

He winced, the picture of her still so clear in his mind. Her lovely, pale, perfect face. The white dress. The red rose.

John nodded. "Seven of us were in there—and seven of us got out quicker than a flash. And we were all interviewed." He sighed loudly. "Hell of a thing for the owner of that place. They've barely been open, what, a month or two? Then they have to stop work and close up because an engineer finds the coffins in the dirt and then the catacombs. They bring us in, and... Sad. So sad. By God, she was beautiful! Poor thing."

"Just to confirm, you were there yesterday?" Craig asked him.

"Of course. I was there as soon as the situation was reported." He paused. "Did you know that the land where the Waldorf Astoria sits was once a potter's field? Think of how old this city is. A number of the parks we enjoy today were originally cemeteries. I worked the old slave cemetery they discovered a few years back, so it was natural that I'd work on this one, too."

"You started on the church yesterday?"

"Yes, I did. I was called yesterday morning and I made arrangements to get there as fast as possible."

"And then?"

"I assessed the location. I called in Digby and my assistant, Allie Benoit. You don't pry apart ancient caskets willy-nilly. We researched church plans, but the original architect's plan is long gone." He shook his head. "You must be familiar with what happened. The church sold the property to the club people. There was an outcry, not that it made any difference. But the building is so historic. Everyone wants to shop Fifth Avenue, see a show, bank on Wall Street. They forget that Wall Street *was* a wall. Canal Street was a canal—or a cesspool, really. Those are all part of our city's origins and we need to preserve history!"

Craig nodded, although he wasn't convinced they'd needed to preserve the cesspool that had been Canal Street. He spoke quickly, not wanting the academic to bluster endlessly. "What time did you get in there?"

"Let's see… They called us right around ten in the morning. I was there within the hour."

"So, who was there then?" Craig asked. "Besides you and the colleagues and workers you've mentioned."

"Oh, lots of people. The manager—owner, too, I think—Roger Gleason. He'd been working down by the construction area. They stored their booze down there—in the old crypt they knew about, I mean, with the coffins and bodies all gone now. It's a foundation, a basement. The basement—the *crypts*—were far more extensive than people realized. The wall had hidden some of the old coffins and shrouded corpses, so when some of the corpses were moved, the 'second' crypt was missed."

"Okay. Anyone else know what was going on?"

"At least two construction workers and one of the barmaid-slash-dancers. Have you seen what they do in there? She was dressed up in a little black bra and skirt and wearing some wicked makeup. The girls dance on tables when they're not handing out booze."

"So, employees, construction workers—anyone else?"

"Oh, yeah, the rep from the historic preservation group. Henry Willoughby. Loves history. He's not a scientist, but he's a great hands-on guy, ready to protect the past and help out if he can. The man loves New York and studied history and architecture. His wife passed away a while back, and now he gives all his love to the city. He stayed long enough last night to check in with us, make sure we were ready to catalogue the bodies and the artifacts we found. I would've brought in more crew, but—"

"Who stayed, then? Who was actually there when you kept working?"

"The seven people you know about—me, Digby showed up, my grad students—plus a structural engineer and a construction worker, all to see that we didn't bring down a wall, I assume." He cleared his throat. "Of course, after I initially went in yesterday, the construction guys created a kind of door for us."

"How long were you there yesterday?"

"Oh, it was almost midnight before I left! I didn't touch or open anything. I stepped over the hole—where the wall broke when they were working on the foundations—into the crypt beyond. We make drawings and assessments and plan before we start the actual work, so, yes, I'd say it was midnight. By then, of course, the vampire dancers were gone and all the club people had been told to go home. Once they'd made the find—

the second crypt—they closed down, of course, but people were hanging around. It's…it's history being reclaimed! Roger Gleason, the owner, seems like a nice guy. He has a conscience and some perspective on what's important. We didn't have to get court orders or anything. He simply agreed to close for a few days. They had patrol officers covering the place, making sure that once the news about the crypt got out, some Goth or necrophilia-pursuing freak didn't try to break in."

Craig nodded. He knew the answers to most of what he was asking; he just wanted it from Shaw and he wanted to ensure that their facts were straight.

"Yesterday," Shaw said, "you understand, it was *discovery* day. I planned where to put some lights. I judged the space for people and decided on equipment. I did all the assessments, got my ducks in a row, you know what I mean?"

Craig nodded again. "This morning when you arrived—were things exactly as you'd left them?" he asked.

"What?"

"Had anything you'd done been changed? Were tools missing, anything like that?"

Shaw frowned. "I… I don't think so. I don't get it. I'd roped off different areas in the basement for my people. We had our little brushes and chisels and…no, I'm positive that our work tables were the way we'd left them," he said. He leaned forward. "Didn't Ms. Gilbert disappear about two weeks ago? She didn't look as if she'd just been killed. She…she was beautiful as she lay there, but some decay had set in. I guess down there, with the cool temperature, natural decay wouldn't be what it would up here." He briefly closed his eyes. "If she was embalmed, she wasn't embalmed really well, but she was…dressed up. As if she'd been prepared for a viewing. Seeing her… It gave me chills! Chills! And I work with the dead all the time. When… when did she die?"

"The medical examiner is estimating her death to have been between one and two weeks ago. He'll tell us more definitively when he's done the autopsy."

"So, you think that…"

"I don't think anything yet," Craig said. "We need more information from the experts before I can even speculate. Go on, please, tell me about this morning."

"Oh. Oh," John said. "This morning." He looked longingly at his whiskey glass.

It was empty.

"You want another?" Craig asked.

"Yeah," John said huskily. "Yeah. The long dead are one thing. Fresh corpses…or not so fresh corpses…"

Craig knew what he meant.

He scanned the bar area but didn't see Kieran. Declan Finnegan, however—looking like an old-time Irish bartender as he dried a glass, decked in a white apron tied around his waist—was behind the bar.

Craig walked over to him. Declan, he knew, had been fully aware that Craig was in the pub and that he was talking to John Shaw.

"You want another whiskey for him?" Declan asked.

Declan was the eldest of the Finnegans; he wore

his sense of responsibility and dignity well. All the Finnegan family were attractive and charming people with different degrees of red in their hair, and they all had eyes in varying shades of blue. Even a casual observer had to note that they were related.

Declan tended to be the most serious in demeanor. He didn't ask questions, not of Craig; he knew he'd learn what was going on if and when it was appropriate.

"Thanks," Craig said. "Any idea where Kieran is?"

"She and Kevin were helping out. I'm not sure where they went. Sorry you had to come to the bar. Anything for you?"

"Soda water?"

Declan quickly poured him a glass from the fountain, and Craig returned to the table. Where the hell had Kieran gone?

She was helping her brother out today, which meant she was working here somewhere. If he was going to start worrying every time she wasn't in sight, he'd have to get a psych evaluation himself.

John Shaw took the whiskey from him; it looked as if he was going to gulp it down. Craig set a hand on his. "Hey, that's prime stuff, my friend. Sip it."

"Yeah, yeah, of course," Shaw murmured.

"Okay, so, you got in today—"

"Early. Just after seven. This is an important true find. The historical value is immense."

"Of course. I understand," Craig assured him. "So, today. You haven't opened any of the other coffins in the catacomb, have you?"

"No. Some of the coffins have disintegrated, and the

remains are down to bones and dust and spider webs. Remnants of fabric… Belt buckles, shoe buckles…" John said, studying the amber liquid in his glass.

"But you found Ms. Gilbert in the first coffin?"

Shaw nodded glumly.

"What made you open that one first?" Craig asked.

The question seemed to confuse Shaw for a minute. "It seemed to be the best preserved…" He paused, staring up at Craig. "Actually, it was at an odd angle on the shelf. As if it had been moved. Oh…that was obviously because someone had been there! They'd put her body in it!"

"Do you remember it being that way the day before?"

"No! That must've been it. There was something different!" John Shaw said. "I didn't realize it immediately. It was such a…subtle difference. The thing is, I thought I'd start with the best- preserved, but so did…" He frowned at Craig. "It was definitely the best preserved. And someone else knew that, too. Her killer."

Jeannette had been dead at least a week, possibly two. But she'd been placed in that coffin in a forgotten crypt much more recently than that.

The killer had learned about the archaeological find—he'd made use of it for his own designs.

"Excuse me," Craig said abruptly. "I'll be right back."

He wanted to see where Kieran was; it suddenly seemed important.

She wasn't at the bar. She wasn't on the floor.

He hurried down the hallway to the office and pushed open the door, not bothering to knock.

Kieran was there, and Craig let out a sigh of relief.

But then he saw that she wasn't alone. She was sitting on the sofa in front of the desk, talking earnestly with her twin brother, Kevin.

They both looked up at him, startled—and their expressions could only be described as guilty.

COMING NEXT MONTH FROM

HARLEQUIN®

INTRIGUE

Available February 21, 2017

#1695 HOLDEN

The Lawmen of Silver Creek Ranch • by Delores Fossen

Marshal Holden Ryland needs answers when his ex-flame, Nicky Hart, steals files from the Conceptions Fertility Clinic—but he never expected to uncover a black-market baby ring or risk it all for Nicky and her stolen nephew.

#1696 HOT TARGET

Ballistic Cowboys • by Elle James

Delta Force warrior Max "Caveman" Decker, on loan to Homeland Security, falls victim to desire on assignment protecting Grace Saunders, a sexy naturalist who witnessed a murder in backcountry Wyoming.

#1697 ABDUCTION

Killer Instinct • by Cynthia Eden

FBI Special Agent Jillian West returns home to the Florida coast after working too many tragic cases, but her former lover, navy SEAL Hayden Black, isn't the only man awaiting her return...

#1698 THE MISSING McCULLEN

The Heroes of Horseshoe Creek • by Rita Herron

Cash Koker has always been a loner out of luck, and when he's accused of murder, he has no one to turn to except BJ Alexander, a sexy lawyer ready to put everything on the line to prove her client's innocence.

#1699 FUGITIVE BRIDE

Campbell Cove Academy • by Paula Graves

Security experts Owen Stiles and Tara Bentley are best friends, but their race for survival against terrorists forces them to confront the true depth of their relationship—the passion simmering just below the surface.

#1700 SECRET STALKER

Tennessee SWAT • by Lena Diaz

Former lovers SWAT detective Max Remington and Bexley Kane have a deeply unresolved history between them, but when they're taken captive by gunmen, addressing the past is the only way for them to find a future together.

SPECIAL EXCERPT FROM

HARLEQUIN®

INTRIGUE

Read on for a sneak preview of
HOLDEN,
from USA TODAY *bestselling author*
Delores Fossen's series
THE LAWMEN OF SILVER CREEK RANCH.

Something wasn't right.

US marshal Holden Ryland didn't have to rely on his lawman's instincts to know that. The Craftsman-style house was pitch-dark except for a single dim light in the front room. The home owner, Nicky Hart, hated the dark, and whenever she was home, every light was usually blazing.

So, either she'd skipped out on their little chat, or… Holden decided to go with the skipping-out theory because at the moment it was the lesser of two evils. After all, there was a reason why they needed to talk.

A bad one.

Holden slid his hand over the gun in his holster and got out of his truck. He'd barely made it a few steps when her white cat came darting out from beneath the porch. It headed right toward him, coiling around his leg and meowing.

Another sign that something was wrong.

Nicky didn't let the cat outside—ever.

Was Nicky inside? And if so, had something happened to her? Holden cursed himself for not having done a silent approach. That way, he could have parked up the street, slipped around to the side of the house and looked in the windows. It might have alerted her neighbors, but that was better than dealing with some of the bad scenarios going through his head. Still, he hadn't taken that precaution because he hadn't figured he would run into any kind of immediate trouble.

Well, no trouble other than an argument with Nicky.

When he'd called Nicky an hour earlier and told her that he was on his way to their hometown of Silver Creek to talk to her, she hadn't said a word about anything being wrong. In fact, she sounded as if she'd been expecting his call. But then she'd sent a text just a few minutes later, saying she wouldn't be available after all.

Right.

Holden wasn't about to believe that lie. She was dodging him. And not doing a very good job of it, either, because her garage door was up, and he could see her car. That meant she was probably inside and that there was a good explanation for no lights on and the cat being outside. He hoped there was a good explanation anyway.

He kept watch around him, kept watch of the house, too, and made his way to the porch. However, before Holden could even ring the bell, the front door flew open, and he braced himself for what he might see.

Don't miss HOLDEN
by USA TODAY *bestselling author Delores Fossen,*
available March 2017 wherever
Harlequin® Intrigue books and ebooks are sold.

www.Harlequin.com

HIEXP0217

HARLEQUIN
A Romance FOR EVERY MOOD